THE BEES OF DEATH

By
ROBERT MOORE WILLIAMS

I0616773

ARMCHAIR FICTION
PO Box 4369, Medford, Oregon 97504

A BUZZING DEATH WAS IN THE AIR!

The future of the entire human race was in serious jeopardy. It all had started with the simple act of an old country bumpkin digging a ditch and finding what appeared to be an old black cannonball. The cannonball certainly looked harmless to the naked eye, only it wasn't really a cannonball. It was something else, and there was something inside it—something alive. And when that something was set free, an unspeakable horror was unleashed upon mankind, the likes of which the world had never known…

Fasten your seatbelts and get ready for a spine-tingling monster-from-the void tale, penned by one of the true masters of science fiction adventure, Robert Moore Williams.

FOR A COMPLETE SECOND NOVEL, TURN TO PAGE 103

CAST OF CHARACTERS

GEORGE GRAHAM
Exposing phony mystics was what he specialized in. What a surprise it was when one mystic turned out to be the real thing!

MILDRED CHAMBERS
She was a high society gal who came to Graham for help. Why did she carry with her the bone-hard corpse of a dead rabbit?

FEATHERSTONE
He was a fake mystic, an extortionist—and he just happened to stumble upon the most horrific creature ever found on Earth.

WITMAN CHAMBERS, III
A powerful man in the world of high finance—but all the wealth in the world couldn't save him from the power within the crystal ball.

LOUIE
Featherstone's assistant. He was loyal to his boss until he found out it could get him killed—by an alien monster no less!

ZEKE
This not-too-bright ditch digger was delighted when he dug up something he thought would put a few extra bucks in his pocket.

CHAPTER ONE

THE BEGINNING was commonplace, stodgy, unimaginative. Necessarily this story must start with a man digging a ditch, a dull, uninspiring, backbreaking task. This was what Zeke Tuttle thought.

He was digging the ditch.

Zeke Tuttle would have preferred to be off fishing, or just loafing in the shade, or doing anything except dig a ditch, but Professor Featherstone wanted the ditch dug, and Zeke, caught without a dime to his name, had agreed to dig it, a fact that he now regretted. It was a hot afternoon and the June sun was broiling down. Added to the discomfort from the hot sunshine was the fact that the ditch had to be dug in hardpan.

Zeke called it hardpan. In reality it was glacial till, although Zeke didn't know this. In the long ago, a retreating glacier had deposited clay, pebbles, and small stones here, and this combination had formed into a compact mass almost as hard as stone. Zeke had heard of glaciers but he didn't know there had ever been any of these huge beds of ice here in New York State. If anybody had told him that 25,000 years in the past the rugged hills surrounding him had been covered with ice a mile thick, Zeke would have called the man a liar.

"Ain't never been that much ice nowhere," he would have said.

Scientific facts had not yet penetrated to the circles in which Zeke moved. One fact, scientific or otherwise, came home with a bang when Zeke's pick uncovered what looked like a cannonball in the bottom of the ditch he was digging.

The object looked like a cannonball, and Zeke was amazed as it suddenly shot into the air . . .

Finding the cannonball pleased him. Professor Featherstone might give him a dollar for a genuine cannonball. Zeke had no idea how a cannonball would get buried under three feet of glacial till.

"Maybe it was shot here in the Revolution," he thought, bending to pick it up.

Swish!

THE CANNONBALL didn't wait for him to pick it up. It jumped out of the ditch on its own accord. It leaped ten feet into the air, then leaped outward and gently came to rest on the ground.

Eyes almost popping out of his head, Zeke stared at it. He had no difficulty in deciding what he was going to do. "Run!" his legs said. He hopped out of his ditch like a rabbit smoked out of its hole, and headed for a patch of trees nearby. For a tall, gawky, ungainly individual, he got up remarkable speed in a short distance. Panting, he dived behind the nearest tree.

He thought he had jarred the cannonball with his pick and it was going to explode. He waited for the explosion. It didn't come. He poked his head around the tree and looked back.

The ball lay on the ground where it had fallen. Zeke watched it for several minutes. Cannonballs were equipped with fuses, he knew, and the fuse in this one might still be burning. He waited ten minutes.

"If she was goin' to explode, she would have already done it by now," he thought. He went back to the ball.

It lay on the ground. He nudged it with his shovel, rolled it over looking for the fuse hole.

There wasn't any hole for the fuse.

The ball was made of lead, he saw. Black lead. The metal had crystallized from age but it was obviously lead. Zeke looked down in the ditch. There was a round pocket where the ball had lain.

He scratched his head.

"Now how in the heck did that thing jump out of that ditch?" he wondered.

He walked around the ball several times, staring suspiciously at it. He stirred it with his toe, rolling it over and over. Since it showed no inclination to do any more jumping, he ventured to pick it up. He got another surprise.

A ball the size of this one, made out of solid lead, ought to have weighed thirty to forty pounds. When he lifted it, Zeke expected it to weigh that much.

It didn't weigh five pounds.

"Must be holler," he thought. He shook it to see if he could hear anything rattling around in it. Nothing rattled. As to what he was going to do with it, there was only one answer: sell it to Featherstone and make himself a buck or two. The professor had been known to buy Indian arrowheads, stones, axes, and knives from farmers who had picked them up in their fields.

Carrying the ball in his hands, he started up the slope of the hill to the house owned by the professor.

"I'll see if I can touch him for five bucks," he decided.

THE HOUSE Featherstone occupied was built on a hillside and was hidden from casual view by a heavy growth of trees. If it had been on level ground it would have been four stories high, but since it was built on a hillside it never managed to reach a greater height than one story. On the first, or lower, level there was a garage, with space for three cars. On the next level, up and farther back on the hillside, were a large dining room and a kitchen. On the third level were a large living room, four bedrooms, and a bath. On the top terrace was a glassed-in compartment designed by the builder as a combination solarium and lookout point.

The man who had built this house had been touched in the head. After Featherstone had finished with him, he had been touched in the pocketbook. In point of fact, to show his profuse admiration for the worthy professor, he had deeded the house and several hundred surrounding acres of hills to Featherstone as an outright gift.

Featherstone had his converts.

Featherstone liked this house. It gave him a place to spend a few restful weeks or months when the heat was on in New York. He also liked it because George Graham did not know about it. From Featherstone's point of view, a hideout that George Graham did not know about was a most desirable thing. Most desirable indeed!

Featherstone was a strange man. If he had been born in central Africa, his calling would never have been in doubt. He would not have been a hunter, a stalker of antelope, a bringer of food to the tribe. He would not have been a fighter, meeting the enemy face to face, a protector of the people. Nor would he have been a worker, a tiller of the soil.

He would have been a witch doctor. The hunters, the warriors, and the tillers of the soil would have brought tribute to him. He toils not; neither does he spin; yet he lives on the fat of the land. A witch doctor, with his face hidden behind a hideous mask, a necklace of lion claws, a cow's tail in one hand and a sack of *grigris* in the other, a worker of dark magic, with fear his chief assistant, and delusion and deceit his stock in trade. Born in central Africa, Featherstone would have been a witch doctor. And he would have been powerful. Whole tribes would have held him in awe, obeyed his commands, served his dark purposes.

If he had been born in Europe in the Middle Ages, he would have been an alchemist, a master of subtle poisons, with a secret laboratory hidden in some dark cave or cellar. In this laboratory he would have sought what so many were seeking in that time—a way to transmute base metal into gold.

In yet other places and other times, he would have been a wizard, a warlock, a magician, trafficking with dark mysteries. And his fate, if caught with the goods, would have been to be broken on the wheel, to be hanged, drawn, and quartered, to be boiled alive in oil. But the odds are he would never have been caught with the goods.

In America, in the Twentieth Century, Featherstone was neither witch doctor, alchemist, nor magician, although he possessed an extensive knowledge of the practices of these trades. Nor was he an astrologer, a fortuneteller, or a cultist. He knew the secrets of the astrologer, the inner workings of the crystal ball, and how to organize and run a cult on the right side of the law. He was not a spiritualist, although he could manage ectoplasm with the best in the business.

There is no one word that could describe Featherstone. He was anything. Although his primary aim was to separate a sucker from ten thousand dollars, he was also willing to separate a sucker from five dollars. If a marked deck of cards would do the job, he used a marked deck of cards. If astrology would handle the separation process, he used astrology. If he found some rich individual, preferably a rich widow who went in for spiritualism, then he brought out his spirits, changing his methods according to the weakness of his victim. He had no scruples, no morals. Honesty was something he liked to find in other people.

This was the man to whom Zeke Tuttle hoped to sell what he thought was a cannonball.

ZEKE FOUND the professor relaxing in the shade of a tree on the highest level of his house, the solarium. He was seated in a heavily padded reclining lawn chair with a tall, cool glass handy to his right hand and a book written by a Hindu philosopher open in his lap. There was a rich widow in Pittsburgh who was interested in Hindu philosophy. Featherstone was reading up on the subject.

Zeke approached, holding the cannonball behind him. "Professor?" he said diffidently.

"What the devil are you doing up here?" Featherstone demanded, noticing his employee. "I hired you to dig a ditch. Why aren't you digging it?"

"I been diggin'," Zeke defended.

"I didn't ask you whether or not you have been digging, I asked you why you're not digging now. I'm paying you to do it, am I not?"

"Yep. You're payin' me."

"Good wages, too. Better than you could get anywhere else."

"Wages are all right," Zeke answered. He was beginning to squirm. City folks had funny ideas about work. When they hired a man they expected him to work from starting to stopping time without taking any time off. Country workers, on the other hand, are accustomed to take time out to rest when they feel the need. In leaving his job, Zeke had not been conscious that he was violating the code governing capital and labor. According to his way of thinking, it was quite all right for a hired man to take time out to go tell the boss something. The fact that he was trying to *sell* his boss something made no difference.

"Well, what are you standing there for?" Featherstone demanded. "What do you want?"

"You wanna buy a cannonball?" Zeke answered, thrusting the object toward him.

Featherstone was a tall man, and even sitting down, an impressive one. He had manner, bearing, sangfroid. In his various occupations, these characteristics were useful. He also had hard black eyes that could turn gimlets to shame.

"A cannonball?" For a moment even Featherstone was surprised. A cannonball was about the last thing on earth he expected to see and certainly the last thing on earth, in heaven, or in hell he expected to buy.

Glancing toward the object his employee had thrust toward him, he saw that it *did* look like a cannonball. He could also see that his employee was trying to sell him something that was already his own property. For someone to sell him something that already belonged to him would irritate him exceedingly. He could see bits of dirt clinging to the cannonball, which indicated that it had come from the ditch being dug on his land. Promptly, he moved to the attack.

"A cannonball, eh? Nonsense. How would a cannonball get here?"

"Maybe shot in the Revolution." Zeke suggested.

"Ridiculous. No battle was fought within fifty miles of this spot."

"Maybe the Indians brought it here," Zeke volunteered. He was feeling a little better. His employer seemed to have forgotten that he was supposed to be digging a ditch.

"Now what would an Indian be doing with a cannonball?" the professor scoffed.

ZEKE COULDN'T answer that question, "Well," he hedged, "It's a cannonball anyhow, no matter how it got here. You wanna buy it?"

"Where did you get it?"

"Found it."

"Where did you find it?"

"Over that way?" Zeke gestured vaguely toward the little valley where he had been digging. He knew as well as

Featherstone where these questions were leading. If he admitted finding the ball in the ditch, the professor could claim it.

"What do you want for it?"

"Five dollars," Zeke answered promptly.

"It's not worth the price but I'll take it." Featherstone pulled a wallet from his coat pocket, and carefully concealing its contents from the inquisitive eyes of his employee, extracted a five-dollar bill from it. He took the cannonball from Zeke's willing hands.

Zeke reached for the bill.

Featherstone snatched it out of his grasp. "I said I'd *take* it, not *buy* it!" he reared, leaping to his feet. "You idiot! Do you think I'm a big enough fool to buy my own property from you?"

"I—" Zeke was startled out of his wits. When the money had appeared, he had thought the sale completed. He now perceived it was not completed.

"You found this cannonball on my property!" Featherstone thundered.

"I—"

"Answer me. You found it in the ditch you were digging!"

"Y—yes."

"Then it belongs to me. Now get the hell back to work. Do you think I'm paying you to loaf around up here in the shade?"

Zeke knew he was licked but he made one last desperate effort to trade.

"Finders keepers," he argued.

"Finders keepers the devil!" the professor snorted. "Anything found on my land belongs to me. I could have you put in jail for trying to sell me my own property. Now get back to work before I dock you for the time you have wasted up here. Get moving. Do you hear me?"

Zeke heard him. He was already moving. Featherstone's laughter came to him as he went down the slope. He was so irritated that he did not tell Featherstone how the cannonball had jumped out of the ditch when he uncovered it. Secretly he hoped the ball would explode and blow Featherstone to hell and gone.

It was a false hope. This ball had never been designed to explode. Quite the contrary.

At that moment, fate must have been sitting back in the wings laughing at the human race. A ball that a ditch digger had found buried in glacial till, a ball that looked like a cannonball but certainly wasn't a ball, that had leaped from the ground of its own accord when freed of the restraining soil, a ball encased in a quarter inch of lead, was in the hands of a man who was potentially the most dangerous crook in the United States.

FEATHERSTONE saw at once that this was not a cannonball.

Through a crack in the lead, he could see something glistening. He cut the lead away, using a pocketknife. Amazement showed on his lean dark face as the object inside the lead came more and more to light.

It was a sphere, of a size that could easily be held in two cupped hands. It was made of a transparent plastic substance that was harder and tougher than any glass he had ever seen. The point of his knife would not even scratch it. Clearly visible inside the plastic, crossed and criss-crossed like the multitudinous threads of a tangled spider's web, was a maze of tiny wires connecting equally tiny instruments.

"A radio set!" he thought. "A radio set in a crystal ball..." Then he shook his head. The instruments inside the sphere looked like they belonged in a radio set but they resembled no radio assembly with which he was familiar. And, among many other things, he had an excellent working knowledge of radio.

The tiny wires all ran to a central core that was about the size of a baseball. This core was black, blacker than the blackest night, so very black that in comparison the best grade of commercial paint would have seemed a drab affair. In that blackness were lights. Millions of lights, an uncounted multitude of lights. Microscopic, almost atomic in size, they danced like incredibly tiny fireflies winging through a summer midnight.

Take a million fireflies and compress them to the size of a baseball. Take their beloved darkness and compress it until it becomes the essence of a thousand midnights. That was the picture of the dance going on inside the sphere and of the blackness in which the dance was taking place. Microscopic fireflies at midnight!

Featherstone frowned in perplexity. "This is marvelous workmanship!" he thought. "Marvelous, indeed."

"Thank you," a voice whispered in his mind.

The sphere had talked back to him!

Featherstone had found a crystal ball that actually worked! Or possibly the ball had found him. It was hard to know which. One fact was clear. A man who was potentially dangerous had in his possession a device that was potentially deadly.

CHAPTER TWO

THE GIRL was frightened. George Graham saw. She was clutching the cardboard box as though she was afraid it would blow up in her face. The furnishings of the office seemed to make her feel a little less frightened. Graham sighed. He wished to hell that sometime he would get a client who didn't pay attention to how the place was furnished. What was it about the human race that made them suckers for an Oriental rug, mahogany furniture, indirect lighting, and a couple of good paintings? Sometime he was going to open an office with nothing in it but a plain pine table, unpainted, two uncomfortable chairs, and a—yes, by Harry—a spittoon; and the client who didn't like the furnishings could get the hell out and stay out.

He rose to his feet. "There is nothing going to jump out of the closet at you, there are no trap doors, I'm not going to hypnotize you or give you drugs. In short, you're as safe in this office as you would be in your grandmother's parlor. So sit down, Miss Chambers, and tell me what you have on your mind."

She forgot her fear in a hurry. Anger replaced it. She had violet eyes. Flames blazed in them.

"I beg your pardon, but—"

"But you are accustomed to having everyone treat you as if you were sugar or salt and might melt if left out in the rain. You are accustomed to having everyone treat you with all the respect due your father's millions. When you enter the presence of a private detective, you expect that uncouth person to leap to his feet, bow from the hips, ask how he may serve your highness."

That ought to fix her, he thought. She ought to swish out of his office with her nose in the air after that speech.

Graham had two reasons for being insulting. One, he was not interested in talking to curiosity seekers. He didn't have time to waste on people who were looking for a thrill. His second reason was more obscure but none the less real. If you insult a frightened person, their fear will sometimes be absorbed in anger and forgotten.

He waited for this girl to react.

She just looked at him. She didn't bounce out of the office. The violet eyes went searchingly, even hungrily over his face. Graham would not have taken a prize in a most handsome or best-dressed man contest but the girl seemed to like the rugged strength she found in his face. Suddenly she sighed, and sat down—wilted down, rather, as though her legs would no longer support her.

"Thank you," she said, "I admit I was—terribly frightened. You did just the right thing to save me from hysteria."

Graham stepped quickly around his desk. It was his turn to be surprised. She had understood why he had talked to her as he had. Not one woman in a thousand would have understood. He decided he liked this girl.

"Sorry," he said, all harshness gone from his voice. "Will you have a cigarette?"

From the thin gold case that he extended toward her, she took a cigarette. He lit it for her.

"Now Miss Chambers," he said, "What can I do for you?"

"You can tell me what to do about this," She handed him the cardboard box she was carrying.

It was a shoebox Graham saw as he removed the paper in which it was wrapped. The girl watched him from frightened eyes as he took off the lid.

Inside the box was a rabbit. A wild rabbit, with long ears and brown fur and a white tail. A common cottontail rabbit. Dead.

THE CLIENTS of George Graham had brought many things to him. They had brought him little dolls with needles thrust into them, they had brought him voodoo charms from Haiti, they had brought him great ouangas that had originally come from Africa. Idols from Tibet, prayer wheels from China, decks of magic cards from Spanish Harlem, all the paraphernalia of superstition, of almost all of it, that the human race had invented. And it had invented plenty!

But no one had ever brought him a dead rabbit in an empty shoebox.

"What kind of a joke——"

The fear on the girl's face stopped him. He swore silently at himself. The black and diabolical designs of superstition may seem silly from time to time but they are never a joking matter. Graham told himself he was old enough and experienced enough to know better than to think someone was playing a joke.

"What is this?" he said.

"A—a rabbit," the girl answered.

"I know. But what else is it?"

"That's—that's what I came to you to find out. You—you specialize in this sort of thing, don't you?"

Graham groaned. "I specialize in exposing fake mediums, fake fortune tellers, fake spiritualists, the tricksters who prey on unfortunate and unhappy people, I do not know what there is to expose about a dead rabbit."

"Look at the rabbit."

"What?"

"Examine it closely. Take it out of the box. Here. Let me——"

Graham caught her wrist, shoved her hand aside. "Let's not touch it unnecessarily," he said. "Wait just a minute. I'll get some gloves."

He went into the next room. There was a laboratory in that room, as complete a laboratory as any in the city of New York. He stayed only long enough to take a pair of rubber gloves from a storage cabinet.

He used these to lift the rabbit out of its box. He set the rabbit on a piece of paper on his desk.

"Now look at it," the girl said.

He saw what she meant. The rabbit sat, naturally on its four feet. There was a suggestion of motion about the little animal. Graham got the impression that this rabbit had been ready to hop when something had happened to it. Instead of moving, the rabbit had been frozen in a hopping position, frozen solid instantly, all motion stilled in the fractional part of a second.

The rabbit had never known what had hit it. There was no indication that it had been fleeing for its life, its fur was not disarranged, and no blood spots were visible. It crouched on his desk ready to hop.

It would not hop again, not ever.

Graham ran gloved fingers over the furry body. The rabbit was as stiff and as solid as bone. He shrugged, slipped it back into its box, then turned to the girl.

"Did you ever see anything like that before?" she asked.

"Never," he answered.

"What do you think it is?"

"I haven't the faintest idea."

Disappointment showed on her face. She had come to him for help and he wasn't doing anything for her. "I thought—"

"You thought all you had to do was to set it on my desk and I would be able to tell you all about it?"

"Something like that," she admitted.

"Thanks for the compliment. I'm neither a superman nor a mental wonder. There are many things I don't know. I don't know, for instance, where you got that rabbit."

HE DIDN'T add that he didn't know enough about her to satisfy him. The Mildred Chambers of the rotogravure section, the Mildred Chambers of the society pages, he knew vaguely. She was a glamour girl, with more money than was probably good for her. She got her picture taken at the Stork Club now with this man, now with that. She lived in the frothy bubble of society, in the false, unreal world of the ultra rich. This much he knew about her from casual reading of the newspapers, but the real Mildred Chambers, the little girl hidden away somewhere behind the false front of the social glitter, he did not know.

He was having the devil's own time connecting the Mildred Chambers, the girl in the ermine wrap whose photograph he had seen in the picture sections, with this frightened, violet-eyed girl sitting in his office, this Mildred Chambers who had brought him a dead rabbit in a shoe box.

He could imagine what a Broadway columnist would make of this situation. He thought of the headline:

SOCIETY GIRL CARRIES DEAD RABBIT IN SHOEBOX

The thought shocked him. It was so fantastic it was utterly horrible. A society girl carrying a dead rabbit around in a shoe box. This in New York City, in the greatest metropolis of the modern world, in the very home of sophistication, in 1949!

Privately, Graham knew that this sophistication was only a thin veneer, that just under the surface of this modern world the old fears of the human race could be found, the fear of the dark, the fear of the jungle, the fear of the evil eye, the fear of plain bad luck. Civilization had veneered man; that was all it had done. Under the skin of New York were all the old, old fears of the race.

"Where," he repeated, "Did you get this rabbit?"

"I found it in my apartment this morning," Mildred Chambers answered. "I called you immediately."

"And where is your apartment?"

She gave an address on Park Avenue. Graham knew the building. It was one of those ultra-expensive places.

"We live on the eighteenth floor," she continued.

On the eighteenth floor of a Park Avenue apartment building she had found a dead rabbit! She lived so high up that the noise of the street did not reach her. She lived up in the clouds almost, in a world set apart from humble dwellers on this earth. She lived in a building of brick and steel surrounded by asphalt streets and concrete sidewalks. Up eighteen stories in the air in a steel and concrete building she had found a dead rabbit. No wonder she was frightened.

"Where in your apartment did you find it?"

"In my father's room."

"Ah. Your father is Whitman Chambers, III?"

"Yes."

"Where in your father's room was the rabbit?"

"Hidden in a drawer of his dresser. One of the maids found it and brought it to me."

"Ah."

GRAHAM THOUGHT what a Broadway columnist would make of this. In the dresser of Whitman Chambers III, wealthy sportsman and descendant of original New York settlers, a dead rabbit had been found. That would be a juicy tidbit indeed. Had the family tree of another original settler developed a nut? Had Whitman Chambers III quietly gone crazy? Keeping a dead rabbit in a dresser drawer was scarcely the activity of a sane mind.

"It isn't that," Mildred Chambers said hastily. "Daddy is as sane as—as you or I. I'm positive of that."

"Did I say he wasn't?" Graham questioned.

"No, but you looked it."

"And you're afraid of it," Graham challenged.

"What?"

"The first thing that popped into your mind when that rabbit was found in your father's room was the thought that your father was going insane."

"No!"

"Isn't the fear that your father is insane the thing you are most afraid of?"

"No, Mr. Graham. My biggest fear is that he is *not* insane!"

Graham walked around his desk, sat down in the chair, and leaned back. The violet eyes of the girl never left his face. The only sound in the room was the soft rustle of the air conditioning apparatus pushing cool air into the room to combat New York's August heat. On the street far below, the honk of a taxicab sounded like a noise from another world.

"If he were insane; you would not be afraid?" Graham said.

"I would be terribly sorry," she said simply. "But I would not be afraid."

He believed her. And he shivered. Out of the corner of his eyes, he was aware of the shoebox sitting on his desk, of the box and of its contents. He felt the cold spidery feet of a nameless dread walk up his spine.

"My father has always been interested in the supernatural," Mildred Chambers continued. "He has an extensive library on the subject. I can't remember a time when some medium or crystal gazer was not coming to our apartment to demonstrate something to him or to try to sell him something. I don't think he ever bought anything except books or ever believed in anything. He frequently said that ninety-nine per cent of the mediums were fakes and that ninety-nine per cent of everything written about the supernatural was obviously nonsense. It was the one medium in a hundred who might not be a fake all the time; it was the one per cent of the supernatural that was true that interested him. I believe he thinks that hidden behind all the false trimmings is a grain of important truth."

Graham nodded, "Most really intelligent people think the same thing," he said. "Most intelligent people are interested in knowing what this world is all about. You have stated my own beliefs exactly. Somewhere there is the truth about everything, about the sun, the stars, and the Earth, and about the life on this Earth. The purpose and the meaning of human life? That is the question. The answer to that question is hard to find. Your father sounds like a man I would enjoy knowing. Go on with the rest of your story."

THE GIRL brightened, "Thank you," she said. "The rest is soon told. About a month ago, my father apparently discovered a part of that grain of truth he has been seeking all his life. At any rate, he found something. A tremendous change came over him."

"What kind of a change?"

"There were two changes. The first one was *eagerness*. He suddenly seemed to find a new zest in life. He was excited all the time."

"Like a child with a new toy?"

"Yes, but it was more than that. For the first time in years, he seemed to be suddenly very much alive. He was glad. He whistled and he sang. He teased me. Then—he changed."

"Yes," Graham encouraged.

"He became afraid, terribly afraid—" The girl groped for words.

"His new toy had turned into a monster?" Graham asked. Again he was aware of the shoebox sitting on his desk, of the shoebox and of its contents.

"Maybe," the girl answered.

"And what do you want me to do?"

"I want you to find out what has happened and to help him."

"I'll take the job, Graham said. "I'll see him tonight."

Surprise showed on her face. "You mean you're going to talk to him? I thought a detective—"

"I'm not the kind of detective who hides in the dark," Graham answered. "I lay my cards on the table face up. I'm going show him this," He pointed toward the shoebox. "And I want you present while I talk to him."

"Me? Why me?"

"For the very good reason that you may have been lying to me," Graham answered promptly. "Or you may have been indulging in a little private fantasy of your own, for reasons of your own. I admit I *think* you're honest and sincere, but I don't know you well enough to be sure of my own conclusions. You may be the nut on the family tree instead of your father."

Anger colored her face. "Do you think *that* is fantasy?" she demanded, pointing to the shoebox.

"That," Graham said, "is the only reason why I am going at all."

He rose to his feet. "I'll see you at eight o'clock."

She didn't like his attitude; she didn't like it even a little bit. She was still angry when she left the office. She would have liked to tell him to go to the devil but her fear was stronger than her anger. He sighed and decided again that she was sincere. And he wished again that he didn't have to hurt people's feelings to get at the truth that was in them. He picked up the shoebox from his desk and carried it into his laboratory.

AN HOUR LATER he was indulging in some fantasy himself. He was apologizing to a person who wasn't present, to Mildred Chambers.

He had dissected the rabbit. Every muscle, every internal organ in the body of the little animal had been stiffened to the hardness of bone.

George Graham had an extensive knowledge of the various ways in which men and animals may die—guns, knives, poison, old age, disease. The rabbit had not died in any of these ways. It had not died in any way that Graham had heard of, or read of, or thought of.

"Whitman Chambers, where did you get this rabbit?" he thought. "And why did you hide it in your dresser? And what devil's broth have you been stirring up, Whitman Chambers?"

Graham was still indulging in fantasy. He had the uneasy feeling that this fantasy was turning into desperate reality.

CHAPTER THREE

WHITMAN CHAMBERS had gray hair and the most penetrating blue eyes George Graham had ever seen. He was a tall man with just the slightest suggestion of a stoop to his shoulders. There was a suggestion of sadness on his face.

"George Graham?" he said, extending his hand, "I have heard of you. Under other circumstances, I would have been glad to meet you."

"I'm sorry you're not glad to see me now," Graham answered. "I'm here to help you. I gather your daughter has told you I was coming?"

They were in a book-lined library. Mildred Chambers, wearing a sleeveless dinner dress, had answered his ring and had brought him to the library where Whitman Chambers waited.

"She told me you were coming," Chambers answered. "I can guess why."

The girl had seated herself in a soft chair. Chambers looked at her. "Would you like to leave me and Mr. Graham alone now?" he asked.

She shook her head, "Mr. Graham insisted that I be present when he talked to you."

"Um?" Chambers looked at Graham. The sleuth nodded.

"May I ask why?"

"Certainly. Your daughter gave me certain information today. I want her to say the same things in your presence that she said when you were absent."

"I see," Chambers answered. He looked angry.

"For her protection, for your protection, and for my protection," Graham added: "I am interested only in the truth."

"You think, perhaps, she lied to you?" Chambers challenged.

"Lying might be one word for it," Graham answered. "It might, however, be better to say that I am not a psychiatrist and I am not interested in the delusions of a deranged mind. She thinks you are in trouble and she hired me to help you. At the time she left my office, I was of the opinion that perhaps your trouble might merely be a delusion on her part. By requiring her to tell her story in your presence, we would be able to tell whether or not it was a delusion. Thus, if she were hallucinating, you would be able to secure the services of psychiatrist rather than a private investigator who specializes in protecting the public from the activities of a certain group of rather unpleasant people."

Graham felt a little uncomfortable. His motives had been honest but they might be misinterpreted.

"You thought she might be crazy, and if so, I ought to know it," Chambers spoke.

"Something like that," Graham answered. He knew the girl's hot eyes were on him but he didn't look at her.

"You have since had occasion to change your mind?" Chambers continued.

"Yes."

"May I ask you what caused you to change your mind?"

"I dissected that damned rabbit," Graham answered.

There was complete silence in the book-lined room. The blue eyes of Whitman Chambers probed into Graham's face, measured him, weighed him. There was fear in the eyes now. Graham could see it lurking deep in the penetrating depths. He had the impression that the man who faced him was keeping his emotions under iron control.

Chambers turned to his daughter.

"So you found it?" he said.

"Yes," she whispered.

As though the strength had suddenly gone out of his legs, Whitman Chambers sat down. A pale film of sweat was visible on his forehead. He took a handkerchief from his coat pocket, dabbed at the sweat.

"Where did you get that rabbit?" the girl spoke.

WHITMAN CHAMBERS rose to his feet, walked across the room, and carefully closed the door of the library. He came back to his chair and he tottered as he walked. He looked at his daughter, then his eyes came back to Graham's face.

"I'm trying to help," Graham said. "I have to know the truth, and the whole truth."

"Man, I know your reputation," Chambers answered. "One look is all I need to see the honesty in you. I know you are trying to help and I know you need the truth. I am not questioning your motives or your need for facts."

"Then what are you questioning?" Graham asked.

"I am not questioning anything," the white-haired sportsman answered. "I am just trying to decide how important it is to me to stay alive."

"What?" Mildred Chambers' sudden whisper was loud in the silent room, "Dad!"

He didn't seem to hear her.

Graham watched in silence. The thousand feet of uneasy fear were crawling on his spine. Chambers' eyes were on his face, never leaving it.

"Dad!"

He still didn't hear her. He looked at Graham, seemed to find strength in the solid bulk of the man, courage in his even, fearless features. There was something about Graham that gave other people courage. Chambers seemed to draw courage from him now.

"I bought the rabbit," he said.

"Bought it?" his daughter questioned.

"Yes. I paid a hundred thousand dollars for it."

Graham gulped. "One hundred thousand dollars!"

That was real money in any man's language. Whitman Chambers III had parted with one hundred thousand dollars to buy a dead rabbit!

"Extortion," Graham said.

Chambers nodded. "You can call it that if you want to. I paid the money willingly and I did not file a complaint with the police. Nor have I any intention of filing a complaint now."

"They got you, eh?"

"They've got me."

"Don't you know they will come back for more?" Paying off an extortionist is just an invitation to him to come back for more money."

"I know that."

"Then why did you pay it?"

"That is a matter between me and my conscience," Whitman Chambers answered. "I do not at this moment choose to reveal why I made the payment."

"Will you tell me the person to whom you paid it?"

"I'll do better than that," Chambers answered. "I'll take you to the place where I paid it and to the people to whom I paid it, I'll let you see what I saw. Then you can judge for yourself whether or not I was justified in what I did. *You* can tell *me* whether or not you think the price was too high. Will you go with me?"

"Of course I'll go with you…" Graham answered.

Mildred Chambers rose from her chair, "I'm going too," she said.

"I would prefer you do not," her father said.

She hesitated, "Can you give me a reason?"

"Yes. It is better for you not to see—"

"What you have seen?"

"Well—"

Shaking her head, she walked over to her father and kissed him. "That's not a good enough reason, I'm going with you."

"Very well," Whitman Chambers assented, "But perhaps—" He looked at Graham.

"I have no objections," George Graham answered. He pressed his left arm against his coat. Yes, the gun was there in its shoulder holster.

Graham's mind came back to a central thought: Whitman Chambers had parted with one hundred thousand dollars. Chambers was no fool. If he spent that much money, he must have been scared right down to the bottom of his soul. What had he gotten in return that was worth a hundred thousand dollars?

Or had Chambers quietly and easily gone batty? There was the rabbit—that triply damned rabbit. The rabbit was dead but it was never under any circumstances insane. It made Whitman Chambers sane too.

Graham swore silently. He had the feeling he wasn't going to like what Chambers was going to show him. He felt of his gun again, to make certain he still had it.

CHAPTER FOUR

THEY WENT in Chambers' car to an address in Greenwich Village, to a neighborhood that had been taken over by people who were trying to be arty. The apartment was on the first floor of a building that looked like it had once been a garage but had been converted into living quarters. Chambers rang the doorbell.

A tall, slender, dark-skinned man with the look of a hawk on his face answered the ring.

"Mr. Chambers. I'm glad to see you. You decided to attend another one of our weekly gathering, I see?"

Then he saw Graham. His face changed.

"Hello, Swami," Graham said, "Or are you using the title of professor now, or perhaps doctor? I haven't seen you in a long time. Where have you been keeping yourself?"

"Hello, Graham," Featherstone answered. There was no pleasure in his voice.

Chambers looked doubtfully from one to the other, "You two seem to know each other," he said.

"Oh, the Swami and I are old friends," Graham said, "Of course. I didn't know I was coming to see him tonight."

"What are you doing here, Graham?" Featherstone said.

"I'm here in the interest of a client," Graham answered promptly. "Are you going to let us in or are we going to have to go out in the street and throw rocks at your windows until you decide to invite us in?"

Graham was assuming a lightness he did not feel. He knew Featherstone, knew him as a master of the art of separating a gullible sucker from a dollar. What was more important, Featherstone knew him. This was a development he had not anticipated.

It was too late to back out now. Featherstone had seen him with Chambers.

Featherstone made no move to get out of the doorway. He frowned at Graham.

"I might have known that sooner or later I would find you butting in on this," he said.

"Does my presence inconvenience you?" Graham asked.

"It isn't that."

"No? Then what is it?"

"It's this. You know some of the hocus-pocus I have used in the past."

"I believe I have heard of one or two little tricks you have used in some of your operations."

"I'm not using any hocus-pocus now. This thing is real!"

For the first time Graham realized that Featherstone was scared, not of the detective, but of something else. *Was it possible that Featherstone was scared of his own hocus-pocus?* Had a faker run into something that wasn't a fake? Had a sleight-of-hand magician found that his magic was working without sleight-of-hand? Had a witch doctor found a death charm that worked?

Or was Featherstone lying, was he putting on an act? That the tall, skinny crook was a first class actor Graham did not doubt. Was he acting now?

"I don't quite understand you," Graham said. "If you have actually made an important discovery, you have nothing to fear from me. On the other hand, the price you are charging for dead rabbits seems a little high."

Featherstone turned his gaze on Chambers. The white-haired sportsman wilted under that hard stare.

"You've been doing a lot of babbling," he said. "You've been working your mouth overtime. The money you donated was a willing contribution and you know it."

Chambers said nothing. All color had left his face.

Featherstone turned to Graham. "You can come in," he said, "And judge for yourself whether the price of dead rabbits is too high to pay."

He turned, led the way into a large studio apartment.

"You—you talk too much," Mildred Chambers fiercely whispered to Graham. "You open that big mouth of yours and everything you know comes out of it. You shouldn't have mentioned that rabbit…"

"Why not?" Graham challenged. "I know this man. He's a faker and a crook."

"But supposing he is not faking, *this time?*"

"Then I have challenged him, and my neck is out a mile."

"And mine too, and daddy's."

"Your neck was already out, baby, and so was your father's. All I've done has been to add mine to the list."

"But—"

"But the minute Featherstone saw us together, we were all on the spot," Graham answered, "He knows me, he knows my reputation, he knows I'm here to show him up if I can. Because I was with you, he knows that either you or your father hired me to catch him. Baby, we're all in this together."

NOT COUNTING Featherstone, there were seven people in the apartment when they entered, four men and three women. There was also a little dog, a Boston Bull, with a round face and a white spot over one eye.

"Sit down," said Featherstone. It was an order, not a request. He left without introducing them to any of the seven people present.

33

They sat down in chilly silence. The four men and the three women glanced at them but said nothing. Graham got the impression that all these people were tensely awaiting something.

The little Boston Bull came and sniffed at his legs. He reached down and scratched it behind the ears. It snuggled up close to him and tried to sit on his feet. He noticed it was trembling. Chambers looked at the dog and his lips closed in a straight line as sharp as the edge of a knife.

The apartment had originally been designed as an artist's studio. The room was huge, with a high ceiling. Broad windows as one had been designed to give light from the north. The windows had been painted black.

Directly under the windows was the strangest piece of furniture in the room, a black box about four feet square. Wooden blocks lifted it a foot above the floor.

Featherstone came back into the room. With him was a round-faced, scar-cheeked, hard-eyed little man who seemed to be his helper.

"Ladies and gentlemen," Featherstone said, "The demonstration I know you are all anxious to see is about to begin. But first I have an announcement to make, an announcement in which I know you will all be interested. We have with us tonight a man who has devoted a major portion of his life to exposing fakes and tricks of all kinds, a man who has boasted that he can duplicate every effect in every séance ever held—"

Graham twisted in his chair.

"George Graham, ladies and gentlemen, is with us tonight. If there is trickery in the demonstration you are about to watch, I am quite sure he will detect it."

Seven pairs of eyes turned toward Graham. He sat as immobile as a rock. The woman with the long cigarette holder looked almost hopefully at him. The thick-necked man in the blue suit gave him a slow stare. Mildred Chambers turned her head and glanced at him.

Featherstone smiled mockingly at him.

"Turn loose your devils, Swami," Graham said, "Let your spirit trumpets blow, let ectoplasm be unloosed."

At his feet, the little dog whimpered in fear.

FEATHERSTONE spoke to his assistant.

"Louie, will you catch the dog."

The scar-faced little man put on a pair of heavy gloves and approached the Boston Bull. It cringed against Graham's feet and tried to jump into his lap. Graham did not know what was going to happen. He let Louie catch the little dog, firmly repulsing the impulse to kick the scar-faced man in the mouth when he bent over to pick up the frightened animal.

"Examine the dog closely," Featherstone urged, "Mark it in any way you see fit."

The animal was passed from person to person in the group. They looked at it with rigid fascination, seeming to see in it the horror normally reserved for a snake. Graham looked at it closely. It was just a little Boston Bull, scared now, frightened by something it sensed was going to happen. Only one person in the group touched it. The thick-necked man in the blue suit took a pair of nail scissors from his coat pocket and carefully clipped a round spot of hair from the middle of its back.

"You are satisfied that you know this animal and recognize it?" Featherstone asked when the examination was complete. All seven nodded.

"And you, sleuth, you can recognize it?" Featherstone said to Graham.

"I imagine I know a dog when I see one," Graham answered.

"Good," Featherstone added. "Louie, will you put the dog into the steel box." He nodded toward the square black box standing on the floor at the far end of the room.

The assistant lifted the lid, dropped the little animal into the box, and closed the lid again. He wasn't rough about it, nor was he particularly gentle. He just dropped the dog into the box as casually as a person might drop a cherished pet a couple of feet to the ground. Graham heard the soft thud as the dog hit the bottom of the box. He also heard its feet pound against the sides as it tried to leap out again.

There was a broad hasp with a heavy padlock on top of the box. Louie locked the lid into place, handed the key to Featherstone who placed it on a coffee table in plain sight of everyone.

Graham was uncomfortable. There was something here that he didn't like, something that he didn't like one bit. He tried to think what it was, and decided it was the casual, impromptu, matter-of-fact manner in which Featherstone and his assistant were acting. Graham had not the faintest idea of what was going to happen, but he had sat through hundreds of séances, he had seen table tipping, and spirit rapping, and had listened to fake mediums relay fake messages from the dead. A factor common to all these performances had been darkness. There had also been a con-sistently strong effort to secure a theatrical effect to impress the audience. The rooms had been draped in black cloth, the mediums had frequently worn turbans; they had covered themselves in black robes. In many instances the audiences had been required to hold hands. They might even have had to sing songs or chant during the buildup.

The buildup had always been there, the bad theater had always been there, strong appeal to the emotions had always been there.

All that was missing here. Featherstone had not tried to impress his strictly limited audience. He had not resorted to any of the tricks of the trade. He was wearing a plain brown business suit that looked like it had been made by an expensive tailor. His assistant was dressed in baggy serge.

FEATHERSTONE had not gone into an act. *He hadn't even turned off the lights!* He grinned sardonically at Graham; he paid the other members of his audience no attention at all. Yet they sat like statues, not moving, scarcely breathing. The woman with the long cigarette holder had nervously stuffed another cigarette into her holder. She was trying to light it and was so nervous she couldn't strike a match.

No one offered to help her.

Featherstone glanced around his audience.

"I can call devils from the vast deep," he said, and paused.

The words were familiar. Graham could not quite place them but they sounded like something out of Shakespeare. The answer, as he recalled the words, was "Why, so can I, or so can any man. But will they come when you call them?"

"They will come," Featherstone stated.

No one spoke.

In the black box at the end of the room, the dog suddenly began to bark.

"I must ask you not to move under any circumstances until I give you permission," Featherstone continued.

The audience sat spellbound. Featherstone's assistant went to the front door and carefully locked it, then stood with his back against the wall.

"Now he'll turn out lights," Graham thought.

Featherstone left the lights burning. The big studio was almost as brightly illumined as it would have been if the noonday sun had been shining into it.

Featherstone turned his back on his audience. He walked to the black box, stood in front of it, and lifted his arms. He was looking up, up at the window that opened out on the night.

On the other side of that window was New York. The blaze of lights in the sky, the honk of taxicabs, the far-off rattle of the elevated railway, all the dim sounds of a great city. New York and the Twentieth Century.

His feet spread wide apart, Featherstone stood with his arms lifted in supplication. The black box in front of him seemed to be an altar and the window seemed to open out on something other than the New York night.

"Come!" Featherstone called. His voice had all the deep impressiveness of a ringing bell.

Something came through the closed window like an arrow from the bow, came out of the New York night, came through the window and into the room.

No pane of glass in the window was broken or otherwise disturbed, but something came through it, came with the darting speed and high pitched drone of a gigantic bee, came darting into the room.

A thin, tinny scream came from the lips of the woman with the long cigarette holder. It was choked off. She stared wildly in the direction of the window, the pulse pounding feverishly in her throat. No one paid any attention to her. No one even noticed that she had screamed. She slumped forward to the floor in a faint and still no one noticed her.

A glacial wind raised ten thousand goose pimples on Graham's body. This—this was his secret fear. In every séance he had ever attended and every trick and fraud he had ever exposed, his secret fear had always been that sometime the séance would not be a trick, that sometime the creature from the shadow world would not be a fraud. The fear had been kept deep in his subconscious mind, unrealized, unknown, a secret cancer that he did not know was haunting him. When the windowpane blurred but did not break, when the vicious whine of that darting bee was suddenly loud in the silent room, his secret fear burst from his subconscious mind and nearly drove him mad.

THE FEAR that hides in darkness, always out of sight, making itself known only by the vague feeling that something is looking over your shoulder, is a hideous trauma, a driving force scourging men to destruction.

Graham's right hand dived unbidden inside his coat, seized the butt of the pistol holstered there. Only the exercise of iron self-control kept him from leaping to his feet.

Sweat trickled down his neck inside his shirt and wilted his collar.

Featherstone stood with arms still uplifted. Little movements of his head revealed that he was trying to watch something in the air.

The vicious whine of a gigantic darting bee was in the air.

Featherstone was trying to follow the movement that had come through the window.

Graham tried to follows its movements too. It was in the room. He could hear it. He could almost see it. Every time he thought he had brought it into focus it darted somewhere else. He caught glimpses of little blurred distortions in the air, little glancing glimmering heat waves.

Now and then he saw tiny flashes of reflected light. They were always gone before he could focus his eyes on them.

He tried to estimate its size. He could not see it clearly enough to tell how big it was. It seemed to vary in size. Now he thought it was as big as a baseball, now it seemed to be the size and shape of a plastic football.

It darted over Featherstone's head and came straight toward his audience.

Hands still uplifted, he turned his head and tried to watch it. On his lean, dark face was the expression of terrific mental strain.

It whined viciously six inches in front of Graham's nose. He couldn't see it. Pain went back along his optic nerve as his eyes tried to bring it into focus, pain as sharp as the shock of an electric current.

It was instantly gone.

It hung in the air before Mildred Chambers. She seemed to have stopped breathing. Her face was ghastly white. It moved on and stopped in front of her father.

Whitman Chambers closed his eyes. He looked like a dead man sleeping. Sweat ran down his face and dripped unheeded from the point of his chin. Then, it moved, and he opened his eyes again.

Graham had the impression he had closed his eyes to avoid the shock of electric pain that came from trying to focus on the thing. If that was true, then Whitman Chambers had seen it before and knew better than to try to look at it.

IT PASSED in front of the other members of the group. Some of them looked at it. Some of them closed their eyes. The woman in the red dress moved bloodless lips in prayer.

It hung in the air in front of the thick-necked man in the blue suit. He stared defiantly at it. This man was not easily intimidated. He had a kind of surly courage that was not easily put down. For a second, he tried to stare. Pain distorted his face. He winced, and closed his eyes.

"Come!" Featherstone said.

The whine darted toward him.

"Accept the sacrifice," he said.

The lid of the black box blurred. The whine of the bee was instantly subdued. It was still audible, but it was much weaker now.

Another sound was in the room.

The sudden howling of a frightened dog!

The little Boston Bull in the box was howling in sudden fear.

The dog screamed its fear. The pounding of its body against the sides of the box as it tried to escape was loud in the room. It yelped and leaped and howled that unbearable horror had come to it. It begged to be released from horror, it tried to escape from its fear, it fought and kicked and screamed that death was better than this anguish.

And stopped pounding against the sides of the box, stopped howling, stopped screaming its horror, stopping asking for—death.

Death found it.

There was not a sound in the room. The woman who had fainted lay where she had fallen.

Featherstone, still standing with his legs wide apart, and his arms uplifted in supplication, spoke.

"You have accepted the sacrifice."

He waited.

"Then go!"

Something came out of the box, whirled once around the room, then went through the window and was gone into the night. A window pane blurred with sudden shifting lights but was undamaged as something went through it and out into the Twentieth Century New York night.

FEATHERSTONE picked up the key from the coffee table and handed it to Graham.

"Will you unlock and open the box?" he asked.

Graham took the key. Featherstone sat down and cupped his head in his hands. He looked desperately tired. His assistant hastened off into a back room.

Mildred Chambers knelt beside the woman who had fainted, began to rub her wrists.

The man in the blue suit stood up. "I'll help you," he said to Graham.

They unlocked the box. Featherstone took no interest in what they were doing; His assistant had returned with a bottle of brandy and Featherstone was pouring himself a drink of that.

The little dog was in the box. Its teeth were bared in a fighting snarl.

It was stiff in death, as stiff as the rabbit had been, bone stiff, stone stiff.

There is terror in unnatural death. There is horror in unnatural death. The fear of unnatural death is one of the fundamental human fears. Death from a known cause is bad; death from an unknown cause is infinitely worse.

Unnatural death had come to the dog in the box.

Graham turned it over. The man in the blue suit seemed to find a horrible fascination in the bare spot on its back.

Using nail scissors, he had snipped the hair from that spot.

"What do you make of it?" he said to Graham.

"I wish I were a life insurance salesman," Graham answered.

"What?" the man gasped.

"I bet I could sell a hell of a lot of life insurance right here in this room," Graham answered.

He turned from the box and walked over to Featherstone.

"What have you got, Swami?" he asked.

Featherstone took another drink of brandy. Graham picked up the bottle and took a drink for himself.

"What have you got, Swami?" he repeated.

"What do you think?" Featherstone answered.

"I'm not thinking right now."

"Um. Did you examine that box?"

"No."

"You should. It's made of steel."

"I'll take your word for that, for the time being. What was that thing?"

"I don't know," Featherstone answered.

"You don't know?"

"No. You can call it a devil, but you are only using a word without saying anything. You can call it an elemental, but again you are only using a word."

"It obeyed you," Graham interrupted.

Featherstone smiled up at him. "Yes, I believe it did," he answered. "I believe it did."

He rose to his feet. "That's all," he said. "That's all for tonight. If any of you want to come back next Thursday night, I will be glad to see you."

He walked out of the room.

Graham let him go. Louie was urging the guests to the door.

"Mr. Featherstone is very tired," Louie was saying. "He can't talk to anyone and he can't answer questions."

Louie looked longingly toward the half empty bottle of brandy. He had the appearance of a man who could use a drink himself.

THE WOMAN who had fainted had been revived. Graham joined Whitman Chambers and his daughter. They walked in silence to the car. When they were in the car, the girl spoke.

"Father, that thing that came into the room—"

"Yes, my dear—"

There was inexplicable fright on her face.

"A few nights ago—I don't remember exactly which night it was—that thing was—was in my bedroom. I awakened and heard it buzzing—"

"I know it was," Whitman Chambers answered.

"You knew it was there!" the startled girl gasped.

"Yes. Otherwise why would I have spent a hundred thousand dollars?"

"What? You spent that money to protect *me?*"

"Of course!" Whitman Chambers answered. "I had attended two of Featherstone's séances. I had seen that thing come through the window one time and kill a cat in that box, the second time a rabbit. Suspecting trickery, I had asked for the body of the rabbit, I was going to have it examined by the best doctors that money could buy. But before I got that done, the thing was in my room at night. I heard it, I heard it disappear. I went to Featherstone. One hundred thousand dollars was the price he asked to control it. He hinted that it had been in your room, and said that a donation would be acceptable. I paid his price without question. I would pay it again without question, my dear—"

"But the police—" the girl protested, "Surely they could have offered some kind of protection."

Chambers sighed. "I have several times one hundred thousand dollars. I have only one daughter. Should I take chances with the police when—when my daughter's life is at stake? No, my dear, this is not something for the police. Do you agree, Mr. Graham?"

"I agree," Graham growled. He could imagine how Chambers' story would have been received in the average police station. The best he could expect would be a gruff. "Brother, you're nuts!" from some desk sergeant. The worst he could expect would be an examination by a psychiatrist. Presuming Chambers was wealthy and influential enough to forestall an examination for mental disturbance (what odd words they used to describe insanity) he could still get himself a reputation for being cracked, but he would not get protection, not from the police, not in a case like this.

THIS WAS something you fought yourself, this was a battle in which neither civilization nor law and order could help you. This was a case of individual survival, of one man and one woman, or of a few men and a few women, against the dark forces of the universe, against the night.

"What do you think, Mr. Graham?" the girl asked.

"I think it's extortion," Graham answered. "Extortion—and something else!"

"Do you really believe it's only extortion?" Whitman Chambers asked. He seemed a little relieved by that thought. If it was just extortion, just a method of prying money out of a wealthy man—

"And something else," Graham repeated. "I know the Swami. He has been a lot of things, and all of them have been crooked. This is crooked too, but the force he is using to extort money out of you is real. And he is scared of it himself. It obeys him, but it also scares the living daylights out of him. That is the most damnable part of the whole case. Featherstone is scared. If he wasn't scared, then there might be some things we could do, but as long as he is scared, we have to walk mighty softly. Because the Swami, whatever else you can say about him, doesn't scare easily."

"What do you think that thing is?" Chambers asked. "The thing that came into the room."

"I haven't any idea whatsoever," Graham answered. "I am fairly familiar with the literature of the occult and there is nothing remotely like it in the maddest dope dreams of the craziest occultist who ever lived. That thing is unique."

He looked out of the car window. The advertising signs of New York glowed in the sky of night. Normally there was solid comfort in all that glittering electricity but there was no comfort in it now. Something else was in that sky, somewhere in that sky.

Graham had visions of a gigantic bee darting and dashing through the sky, twisting and turning in the night, buzzing as it moved. He visualized it leaping out toward the moon, maybe out toward the stars.

"What do you think we ought to do?" Mildred Chambers asked.

"How about taking a quick trip to Europe and forgetting to come back for a couple of years?" Graham suggested. "That ought to solve your problem for you. Featherstone will scarcely follow you to Europe."

There was silence.

"What about you?" Chambers asked.

"I'll stay here and see what can be done," Graham answered.

The silence fell again.

"We run while you stay and fight," the girl said.

"Well—"

"No thanks," she answered. "We don't run off and let somebody else fight our battles for us."

"Good girl," her father said.

"Graham was glad he had already decided he liked this violet-eyed girl.

Actually I don't see where you are in much danger now," he said. "You have already paid off. Featherstone should let you alone now."

Their silence told him that they knew as well as he did that he was lying. In dealing with an extortionist, the pay-off is no protection. There were two good reasons why all three of them were in danger. One, they knew too much. Two, Featherstone was scared.

CHAPTER FIVE

GRAHAM left Mildred Chambers and her father at their apartment. He didn't even go up with them. They would want to talk and he had nothing to talk about, as yet. He wanted to think. He had the definite foreknowledge that his thoughts were not going to make him happy but he had to think them anyhow. He decided to walk back to his own modest bachelor apartment. It was almost midnight. Featherstone's séance—Graham used that word in the absence of a better word to describe what had taken place in Featherstone's studio—had not taken much time. The Swami had not attempted to put on a show. He had gone directly to the point and if the audience didn't like the shortness of the demonstration or the abrupt way they had been booted out when the performance was over, they could lump it.

Graham caught himself watching the sky as he walked down the almost deserted streets. The night was pleasantly cool for August in New York. The moon was over Manhattan. The old town looked quiet, peaceful, and serene. It was hard to realize there were places like Featherstone's studio in a town that looked so comfortable and placid.

"What in the name of heaven is that thing?" Graham thought. "It came through the window and the glass blurred but did not break. It went into that steel box and killed the dog—"

He was cold, cold, *cold!* It had killed the dog. Of course he hadn't examined the box. He only had Featherstone's word that it was made of steel. But Featherstone had invited him to examine it and he was willing to bet that if he had looked it over, he would have found it was actually made of steel. Of course, there might be a trick of some kind. An X-ray machine might be hidden in the room under the box, its radiations focused to pass through the floor and through the box, but he knew of no X-ray, nor any other kind of ray, that would turn a frightened dog into bone.

There wasn't any ray like that. Or if there was, it was the product of some obscure inventor who had never let his discovery become known.

There might be an inventor who had done exactly that. And Featherstone might have gotten control of his invention.

"Maybe I better pay a quiet visit to Featherstone's studio and see what I can find out," Graham thought. "I might discover something. I also might get my tail full of lead, but I sure as hell don't know where else to start."

The absence of a starting point was giving him more trouble than anything else.

HE BOUGHT a paper, went into a restaurant for a cup of coffee and a ham sandwich. Graham was a confirmed believer in combining reading and eating. When he reached the third page of the paper, he stopped eating.

A feature story on page three gave him a starting point. The story had originated in the town of Elm Point, which Graham remembered as being a small town about two hundred miles from Manhattan. It had been written by some special correspondent and was dated the preceding day. The headline read:

FARMER'S COW TURNS INTO BONE

Elm Point, N. Y., Aug. 21 (Special) Sam Wakely, prominent farmer living near here, went out into his barn lot yesterday morning and discovered that one of his cows had mysteriously turned into bone over night. According to Wakely, he found the animal, a fine Jersey, standing stiff and cold in the corner of the barn lot when he went out to do his morning feeding. Although dead, the cow was still on her feet, but toppled over when Wakely pushed against her side.

James Watkins, Elm Point veterinarian summoned by Wakely, says that he has never encountered a similar case in his extensive experience as an animal doctor. He professes himself to be completely baffled as to the cause of the condition.

A rabbit and a dog in New York. In Elm Point, two hundred miles away, a Jersey cow.

Graham found a telephone. After some argument with a sleepy central in Elm Point, he finally got Watkins out of bed.

"Most amazing thing I ever saw," the veterinarian said. "Most amazing thing I ever saw. You with a New York paper, you say? Well, that cow was dead and I don't have the slightest idea what killed her. Fine Jersey, too.

"Huh?

"City man, you say? Name of Featherstone? Let me think—"

Graham hung on to the wire while the sleepy veterinarian shuffled through his mind.

"I believe there is a man by that name living around here. Come to think of it, I believe his place joins Wakely's farm on the north. You looking for him to add something to your story, maybe?"

"Thank you," Graham said, and hung up.

Featherstone had a place in Elm Point. There was a dead cow in Elm Point.

GRAHAM headed directly for his apartment. He intended to dump some clothes into a suitcase, pick up his car at the garage, and take off for Elm Point. The elevator operator in his building recognized Graham. The operator was colored. He was also a little scared.

"Evenin', Mr. Graham. Been somethin' buzzin' around in this here lobby."

"What?" Graham said.

"Somethin' like a big bee, I heard it and I heard and I heard it, but I ain't never seen it at all. What's the matter, Mr. Graham? Ain't you all goin' up to your apartment after all?"

"I forgot something," Graham answered. "I got to go back and take care of it."

He went through the lobby and out of the building in one hell of a hurry.

He wondered what he would have found waiting for him if he had gone on up to his apartment.

If anything followed him, he did not see it.

GRAHAM saw Wakely's cow. It was the middle of the afternoon when he reached the farmer's place.

He had driven all night and had registered in a hotel in a town about twenty miles from Elm Point. For obvious reasons, he did not want to be seen around the latter place.

Wakely was a middle-aged farmer. He was a little scared but not too scared to have his business eye wide open. He charged Graham a dollar to see his cow.

Graham needed only a minute to determine that the cow, the dog, and the rabbit had died from the same cause.

"She was standing right where she is now when I came out of the house in the morning," Wakely said. "All the other animals was herded together up in the corner of the lot. I thought maybe a wolf had scared them during the night. There's still a few wolves around here. It's mostly cutover timberland from here to Canada and now and then a few wolves come down from up north. But it wasn't no wolf that killed her."

"I can see that," Graham answered.

"I called Doc Watkins and he come out and looked her over. He charged me two dollars, which was plumb wasted 'cause there wasn't anything he could do."

"You have any idea what killed your cow?" Graham asked.

"I haven't an idea in the world," the farmer answered.

"Well, thanks," Graham said, "Incidentally, doesn't a man by the name of Featherstone own the adjoining farm?"

"Yeah. City feller. From the next bend in the road you can see his house."

Graham caught a glimpse of Featherstone's house as he drove past. He didn't stop. He saw a gang of workmen busy cleaning up the debris left over after the construction of a large barn-like structure next to the garage. A new power line had been strung from some distant source of electric current to this building. Heavy transformers on the last pole of the high line fed current into Featherstone's new construction.

Graham frowned. Featherstone was building something. It was out of character for the Swami to make extensive additions to his property, especially expensive additions. The price of high lines and big transformers was more than hay. What was Featherstone building?

It was a passing question. Graham had other and more important questions to think about. One question was why Wakely's Jersey cow had been killed. Extortion could not be involved. The farmer didn't have enough money to interest Featherstone. Probably even the threat of death would not jar him loose from his hard-earned dollars. Farmers were likely to be independent as the devil. No, the Swami was not trying to extort money from Wakely. Then why had the cow been killed?

One possibility was that the farmer knew too much and was being warned to keep his mouth shut.

"That doesn't make sense either," Graham grumbled.

OBVIOUSLY Wakely *hadn't* kept his mouth shut. He had called a veterinarian, had talked to the newspapers. If the death of his Jersey had been intended as a warning, Wakely would have known enough not to talk about what had happened.

No matter how he looked at it, the death of the cow had all the appearance of an accident.

"I wonder if Featherstone knows that cow is dead," he barely whispered.

The thought scared him. He was scaring easily these days and this thought scared him again. Didn't Featherstone have full control of the thing that had come through the window and killed the dog in the steel box? Had it slipped away from him and gone on a killing spree of its own, its victim being Wakely's cow?

Graham clearly remembered the fear that Featherstone had shown during his séance, the suggestion of strain visible on his lean face as he called his devil not from the vast deep but from the infinitely more vast sky. Was that fear rising from the knowledge that he could not guarantee control of the monstrosity he could evoke?

"I wish I lived on an island in the South Seas!" Graham thought, "I wish I was a beachcomber and had nothing bigger to worry about than when the next coconut would fall from a tree."

He drove back to the town where he was staying but he didn't go near the hotel where he was registered. Maybe he was shying from shadows but he intensely disliked visiting the same place twice. Something might be waiting for him if he went back the second time.

For a hard-boiled detective, who had spent most of his life exposing fakes, who believed nothing that he read and little that he saw, Graham was developing a set of nerves.

He went to a clothing store and bought a pair of overalls, a pair of tennis shoes, and a dark cap. He went to a hardware store and bought a light crowbar and half a dozen plain corks, which he placed in his car. He bought a paper to read while he was eating dinner.

It was on the first page.

NOTED FINANCIER DEAD
Whitman Chambers III Victim of Mysterious Attack
DAUGHTER MISSING

Graham didn't eat any dinner. By midnight that night, wearing the rough clothes and the tennis shoes he had bought, his face and hands darkened with black cork, he was in the little valley below Featherstone's four-level house.

A NIGHT wind came slowly up the little valley. It rustled the leaves of the trees with an infinity of scratchy sounds. It was a cool wind, too cool for August, and it seemed to be moving in from outer space and trying to hug the Earth for warmth. Overhead the stars glimmered in the night, pale dots of light in comparison to the brightly shining moon.

Graham did not know whether or not he liked that moon. The moonlight helped him to see where he was going. On the other hand, it might make it easier for him to be seen. His dark clothes would reflect no light and the cork on his face and hands ought to make his skin invisible but he had the unhappy feeling that there *might* be something here in this place that could see in darkness.

A light was visible on the third level of Featherstone's hideout. The new building that had been constructed beside the garage was dark. There were no windows in this building and only one door. The door was sheathed in sheet steel, Graham discovered, as he came cautiously around the building. He didn't try to open the door. He listened. Hair raised along the back of his neck.

The building sounded like a beehive.

Through the steel door, he could hear a muted humming, a buzzing, like the buzzing of a swarm of bees. Notes rising suddenly sharp and shrill were like the quick darting of individual bees testing their wings in flight. In the background was the steady hum of the swarm.

The sound of big bees!

Hackles of tiny hair rose all over Graham's body as he listened. The oldest fear of man, the fear of unnatural death, pounded with his bloodstream through his body. Natural death was bad enough but through familiarity the mind had learned to accept natural death as inevitable, but unnatural death the mind of no man had yet learned how to accept.

Bees that were not bees, big bees, bees that moved too fast for the eyes to follow, bees that came through a closed window, blurring the glass, bees that went through a steel box, blurring the sides but leaving no mark of their passing.

Had Whitman Chambers heard the sound of a bee before he died? Or had the bee come too quickly for him to hear it?

Would George Graham hear the sound of a bee before he died? Would the rapid darting of an angry bee roar in his ears just before his body froze?

The door of the building scraped as it started to open.

Graham slid back into the shadows.

Featherstone came out of the door. Louie, his assistant, followed him. Louie closed but did not lock the door.

"One more load and we'll have everything moved in here," Featherstone said. "Between you and me, Louie, I'll be damned glad when we get this job done."

"You and me both," Louie fervently answered. He looked furtively around and his voice dropped to a whisper. "Do you think we can get away from here tomorrow?"

"Don't ever say that!" Featherstone hissed. "Don't even *think* it!"

Featherstone glanced quickly over his shoulder at the closed door. In the moonlight his face was haggard and old.

Except for the heavy hum of the power transformer on the pole at the end of the building, there was no sound. Featherstone cocked his head and listened. The night wind went softly past, rustling the leaves of the trees.

"Come on," Featherstone said, his voice unnecessarily loud as if he spoke for the benefit of unseen listeners. "We still have work to do tonight."

CHAPTER SIX

GRAHAM stared in dumfounded amazement after them as they stalked up the hill toward the lighted room. His amazement abruptly grew to startled incredulity when he saw the girl step out of the shadow of a tree and say:

"Hands up…"

He knew that girl, would know her anywhere he heard her speak. Mildred Chambers! Missing in New York, present here, present with a gun in her hand! Present, and talking like a highwayman, briskly saying, "Hands up!" over the threat of a gun. He admired her courage. It was a splendid thing, much better than her judgment.

Both men quickly lifted their arms. Then Featherstone recognized the girl behind the gun.

"Miss Chambers!" he said.

"That's right," the girl answered.

"What are you doing here?" he asked.

"I came after you," she answered.

"After me?" There was astonishment in his voice. "May I ask why?"

"As if you didn't know!" Hot bitterness surged in Mildred Chambers' voice. She came closer to him, the gun held very steady. "You—you murderer…"

"What?" Featherstone gasped.

"Walk up that path," the girl ordered. "Keep your hands in the air, both of you."

She started to slip past them on the sloping hillside. Her purpose was to get behind them and force them to walk up the path ahead of her.

Her foot slipped on the steep slope.

As she tried to catch herself, the gun momentarily pointed down. Featherstone reached out a long arm and snatched it from her grasp. Louie grabbed her. She squealed, tried to scream. Louie's hand clamped over her mouth.

Skirts flying in the air as she tried to kick herself free, the two men carried her through the lighted door.

Graham had already made up his mind. She had asked for trouble when she came here. A little rough handling would hurt nothing but her dignity. Before he went up and rescued her, he wanted a peek behind that steel-sheathed door.

He opened the door the tiniest crack. The sound of darting bees was loud in his ears.

A spray of light was flooding up from a dark receptacle in the far corner of the building. The light was an intense violet color, so violet that it hurt the eyes. The bees were playing in the spray of light.

There were four or five of them. Moving faster than the eye could follow. Graham could not count them. He could see glimmerings of flashing light darting into and through the spray of up-flung violet illumination.

Feeding, playing, bathing? He could not tell. The things were doing something, he did not know what. Featherstone's devils. Like the devil that had come through the window of the Swami's New York studio, that had come out of the night. Graham seemed to hear again the howling of a frightened little dog. Five devils. Playing in violet light. Graham's eyes began to hurt as he stared at them, tried to follow their darting motion.

FLASHING in and out of the violet glow, they were as beautiful as humming birds playing in a sunbeam. He would have been entranced by the sight, if—if a frightened dog had not kept howling somewhere in the back of his mind.

The building in which they were playing was a single room. Wooden posts supported the roof. Workbenches were built along two sides. The whole structure had the appearance of hasty improvisation. It was crammed almost to the roof with electrical equipment.

Part of the equipment appeared to have been put into place and the building erected around it. Looking at the building and especially at the electrical equipment in it, Graham could easily guess where a good part of Whitman Chambers' hundred thousand dollars had gone.

Graham looked for only an instant, then softly closed the door. He had the feeling that he had risked his life a dozen times over in opening the door for only a second.

He slipped silently up the path to the lighted window. Mildred Chambers was sitting in a chair. Featherstone was standing in front of her.

"You called me a murderer," Featherstone was saying. "What did you mean by that?"

"You killed my father," the girl answered. Graham wondered if she had gone hopelessly crazy. People who had good sense didn't call murder by its right name when they were in the presence of the murderer and in his power.

Featherstone looked blank. "Are you mad? I killed your father? That is ridiculous nonsense. I haven't seen your father since he left my last séance and he was in good health when he left my studio."

"You killed him just the same," the girl insisted. "The same way you killed the dog."

"What?" Featherstone's blank look deepened.

"You did it. I found him myself. Oh, I know you probably can't be legally convicted of the crime, but you're guilty just the same."

Featherstone stared at her. "Now, now, child," he said soothingly. "I know you are all mixed up and confused and frightened. You are imagining things, aren't you? Come now...tell the truth. You made up this fantastic story, didn't you? You can tell the truth. No one is going to hurt you."

Mildred Chambers stared at him in utter bewilderment. "You—you talk as if you don't know what happened!"

"I'm sure nothing happened, child. I'm sure this is only your imagination."

"Don't—don't you ever read the papers?" she asked.

Surprise showed on his lean face. He looked quickly at his assistant. "Louie—"

"They're over there on the table," Louie answered. "I brought them from the mail box this afternoon but you were too busy to look at them."

Featherstone snatched the still unrolled newspaper from the table. His fingers shook as he tore it open. He glanced at the front page.

As he read the news story, Featherstone began to look more and more like an old man. The fire of life, the zest for living, went out of him like air cut out of a punctured toy balloon.

Graham saw how preoccupied Featherstone was with the story in the paper. He opened the door and stepped quietly into the room.

"Is it that bad, Swami?" he asked.

MILDRED Chambers took one look at him and screamed. To her, he looked like a ghoul coming unobtrusively out of the darkness.

He had forgotten the burnt cork daubed on his face and hands.

"Take it easy, baby," he said.

She recognized his voice and flew to him. His eyes on Featherstone and Louie, he drew his gun.

"Don't either of you get any ideas," he said.

Louie, his eyes on the gun, halted the sudden flash of his hand toward his coat pocket.

Featherstone glanced up from the paper, blinked at Graham, then continued reading.

Graham stared at him. "His most dangerous enemy comes into the room with a gun in his hand and he doesn't even notice," he whispered.

"What?" Mildred Chambers said.

"I come in here and pull a gun and Featherstone doesn't even pay any attention to me," he said.

"Do you feel slighted?"

"Do you know any prayers?"

She stared at him like she was trying to see through the cork and make certain it was actually Graham underneath.

"You better be saying them, if you know any to say," Graham answered. He watched Featherstone, never for an instant taking his eyes off the man. Out of the corner of his eyes, he watched Louie.

Still unaware of Graham, Featherstone finished reading about Whitman Chambers and the way Whitman Chambers had died. Casually, without seeming to notice what he was doing, he laid the paper on the table. His mind was full of another thought. He looked again at Graham and did not see him. He started toward the door, turned and took three steps in the opposite direction, turned again.

He was pacing the floor.

Suddenly he spoke.

"Graham, how did you know I was here?"

"Um. That's not a hard question. There was a story in the papers about a cow that had turned to bone—"

"What?"

"She turned to bone just like the little Boston Bull in your steel box. I thought you might be somewhere near the place where that happened—"

Featherstone had stopped listening. He was pacing the floor again.

"Graham, are you telling the truth?"

"I saw that same story," Mildred Chambers whispered. "That was how I traced him too."

Graham said nothing.

Featherstone abruptly sat down. He looked at Mildred Chambers.

"You may believe me or not, as you choose, but until you told me, I knew nothing of the death of your father."

Graham took a deep breath. He slipped the pistol back into his pocket. "That's what I was afraid of," he said.

"You may well be afraid," Featherstone answered.

"You can't control your devils?" Graham said.

"I can't control them," Featherstone admitted.

"I'M AN extortionist," Featherstone said. "I'm a faker, I'm a charlatan, I'm a crook. But I'm not a murderer, no—"

"I believe you gave Whitman Chambers the impression that unless he paid off his daughter—"

"Gave him the impression, yes," Featherstone interrupted. "I have admitted extortion. But if Chambers had laughed at me, I would have sought out some other wealthy person to scare money out of. That was the purpose of my weekly séances. I had no intention of carrying my threats."

He shook his head. "Terror, not murder, is my business. No one ever succeeds in washing the stain of blood off his hands, I did not kill Whitman Chambers."

"You admit that the—for lack of a better word I must say the devil over which you have—or had—at least partial control could have been used to kill him," Graham said.

"Lord, yes!" Featherstone shivered. "I admit that I could—and possibly still can—use it to kill anyone anywhere. But, except for animals, I did not use it for that purpose."

"You did not send one of them to kill Wakely's cow?" Graham questioned.

"I did not," Featherstone answered promptly. He turned his black eyes on Graham. "How did you know there was more than one of them?"

"I looked inside the building at the foot of the hill," Graham answered.

"You did!"

"Yes."

"And you're still alive!" The words were spoken in a wondering whisper. Featherstone looked at Graham, then looked away. His forehead creased in thought.

"I don't understand *that,*" he said.

"You mean you don't understand why I'm still alive?" Graham questioned.

"That's right. Surely the *draal* was aware of you, even before you opened the door—"

He came over to Graham, looked wonderingly at him, reached out a hand and touched the private investigator. When he spoke, he seemed to be talking to himself.

"Was the *draal* asleep? No, that's not possible, I don't think it ever sleeps. Then why didn't it know you were outside the building and why didn't it kill you?"

"Eh?" Graham said. The thousand feet of naked fear walked over his skin.

"You should never have been able to approach within a hundred yards of that building. You should never under any circumstances have been able to open that door."

Featherstone spoke like a man in a trance.

"You opened that door and you're alive," he continued, "I wonder—I wonder if the *draal* knew you were there, but did not want to kill you until you were somewhere else? I wonder why you're still alive? Tell me, did something follow you away from the building, did something follow you up here?"

"Something like what?"

"Something that sang like a big bee when it moved."

Graham shuddered. "Not that I was aware of," he answered.

"Then I don't begin to understand it," Featherstone said.

"Why don't you let someone help you understand?" Graham suggested.

Featherstone's black eyes centered on him. Graham wondered when this enigmatical crook, this self-confessed extortionist and faker, was going to talk. Featherstone had admitted extortion but extortion was only a small part of a much bigger story. When was Featherstone going to reveal the whole story?

When was he going to tell what those five glinting creatures playing in the spray of violet light were?

THE STORY belonged to Featherstone. He could reveal it or keep it to himself, as he chose. Neither force nor threats would move him.

Graham was desperately eager to know the whole story. The fact that his life might depend on his knowledge was not the only reason he wanted to know. All his life he had been trying to lift the veil from the face of truth, to glimpse if only for a moment something to the dark reality of the universe. Featherstone had discovered something. Graham wanted to know what it was.

"What for instance, is the *draal?*" he questioned.

He kept the tone of his voice calm; he kept his words matter of fact. He was trying to nudge Featherstone into talking.

Featherstone was in mental turmoil and Graham knew it. Every action of the man indicated an intense mental conflict going on within his mind. He looked like a man in a trance. He had shuddered away from the suggestion of murder, yet he must know that he was at least partly responsible for the death of Whitman Chambers. This was one cause of the conflict in his mind. He had admitted extortion, he had admitted he was a crook, a faker. A man who will make such admissions is trying to make up his mind to admit even more. Graham was trying to help him make up his mind.

There was silence. Louie had sat down and was nervously smoking a cigarette. Mildred Chambers watched, her face tense with unexpressed fear. Far off in the night a car honked. Off there somewhere in the darkness somebody was driving a car along a road, somebody who had never heard of a *draal*, who had never seen five weird incredible devils playing in a spray of violet light.

"I'm trying to help you," Graham gently said. "I think you have discovered something that turned out to be bigger than you thought. I'm trying to help you get out of the hole you're in."

There had been hostility in Featherstone's eyes. A little of the hostility went away when Graham spoke. But the grim central core of his thinking did not change.

"I believe you," Featherstone said. "Odd as it, I believe you would actually help me if you could."

"I can try," Graham said. "I think I told you once before that you had nothing to fear from me, if you had made me an honest discovery and were using it for honest purposes."

"I wasn't using it for honest purposes."

"When you are willing to admit that, I am willing to help you. What is a *draal*? I would like to know."

"The *draal*?" Featherstone paused. Graham had the impression that the man was listening before he answered. His face was tense, his eyes alert.

The night wind went over the roof of the house, softly sighing. Featherstone looked up, listened to the wind, made certain it was *only* the wind, before he answered.

When he spoke his voice was the lowest possible whisper.

"The *draal* is a brain!"

He looked quickly around the room as if he was afraid someone was listening.

"A brain?" Graham spoke.

"Yes. Speak in a whisper, will you? It probably doesn't make any difference but I feel a little safer when we speak softly."

CHAPTER SEVEN

THE WIND, blowing through an open window, tugged at a curtain. Featherstone's gaze concentrated with terrible intensity on that moving piece of cloth.

"It's only the wind," he muttered at last.

"You were telling me about...the *draal?*" Graham whispered.

"Yes. So I was. So I was. The *draal* is a brain—" He paused, groping for words. "When I say the *draal* is a brain, I don't mean that it's like a human brain. It isn't. The only parallel between the *draal* and the human brain is that both of them are organs capable of rational thought. The parallel ends there. There is no comparison between the quality of the thinking of the two organs. So far as I have been able to determine, the thinking power of the *draal* begins at about the highest level of which the human mind is capable."

Again he looked around the room, seeking some invisible listener whose presence he suspected but could not detect.

"Where did this brain come from?" Graham questioned.

"It was found in a ditch," Featherstone answered.

"A—!" Graham abruptly shut up. He looked closely at Featherstone, seeking the telltale marks that would reveal a wandering mind. A brain found in a ditch! It seemed incredible.

"It was in a plastic ball that was incased in lead," Featherstone continued. "How long it had been in that ditch, I do not know, but it must have been there for thousands of years. It was covered with compacted glacial detritus that must have been deposited during the last ice age."

He began pacing the floor again as he sought the answer to some perplexing problem.

"I have thought and thought about the origin of the *draal*," he continued, still speaking in a whisper and still keeping a wary eye on the blowing of the curtain at the window. "And I have not reached a conclusion. If it originated on Earth, then there must have been other pre-human races of tremendous intelligence on this planet. I think a far more likely solution for its origin is that it came from somewhere in space, and reaching Earth just as the last ice age was ending, was somehow caught and buried in a flood of water flowing from a glacier."

Graham was silent. Was Featherstone telling the truth or was he putting on a superb act, building fantasy on fantasy, erecting a towering dream structure of other worlds and other universes? Graham was not certain, but more and more he was beginning to suspect that the faker was telling the truth. Certainly Featherstone's words were opening long avenues into space and time, were revealing tantalizing glimpses of the secrets that went into the making of the worlds.

"Another problem I have not been able to solve," Featherstone spoke again, "is whether the *draal* is itself an independent brain or whether it is only the relay station of some other greater brain that's located somewhere else."

"Ah," Graham said.

FEATHERSTONE'S piercing eyes were on him. "You think you have a brain," he said. "And you think your thoughts originate in your brain. Did it ever occur to you that your thoughts might not be your own, that your brain might be only a relay station receiving impulses from some infinitely greater, mightier, stronger brain located perhaps even outside space and time as we have come to know them?"

Graham stared at this enigmatical man. "And I thought you were just a crook!" he whispered.

"I am a crook," Featherstone answered. "But not *just* a crook."

"I'll say you're not! Did you know that when you talked about the human mind being only a relay station operated by some greater mind you were coming very close to some of the most advanced scientific thinking of this century?"

"Of course I know it," Featherstone answered.

"I think," Graham said slowly. "I think perhaps I'm beginning to trust you."

"You have to trust me," Featherstone answered, "And so does this girl. And so does Louie. And so does the whole damned human race tonight."

"What?"

"Haven't you yet realized what those things down in that building mean?" Featherstone asked.

"I'm beginning to realize it," Graham answered grimly. "I didn't realize it at first, because I thought you could control them."

"I'm not at all certain of my control. At first, when there was only one of them, I was sure of my control. That was what led me astray. I was tricked and didn't know it."

"I guessed something like that. And I didn't know whether to shoot you or help you."

"The time when shooting me would do any good is passed," Featherstone said. "If you had shot me two months ago, it might have done some good. I say *might*. Probably, if I had been taken out of the picture, the *draal* would merely have fastened on someone else and the result would have been the same whether I was living or dead. No, Graham, this is no time to shoot me. I'm the one man on earth who has to stay alive until—"

He paused, then said, "Until it is determined whether or not the human race is to remain the dominant species on this planet."

Mildred Chambers had been following this conversation in silence. Changing emotions showed on her face as she listened now to Graham and now to Featherstone. Doubt, disbelief, uncertainty, had all from time to time showed on her face. Disbelief showed on it now.

"That sounds silly," she spoke. "Those devils may be dangerous, they may be deadly, but there are only a few of them, only as many as I have fingers on one hand. There are hundreds of millions of men. How can four or five creatures, even with tremendous powers, overcome the millions of humans?"

Featherstone looked at her. "I wonder what dinosaurs thought when a little animal something like a shrew squeaked at them around the edges of their marshes, hopping frantically away from their thundering feet? If the dinosaurs had been capable of thinking, I wonder if they would have thought silly the idea that the far-removed descendents of this little shrew might sometime supplant them? There were millions of them. Any one of them could have crushed the squeaky little shrew without knowing it. Yet the dinosaurs are gone and the descendents of the shrews rule this planet today."

He shrugged. "Evolution and survival are the only different words for battle. You are either stronger, smarter, or swifter than something else—or you die. That is one of the fundamental laws of the universe. And you cannot evade the fight. The human race has fought the battle of evolution since this planet cooled enough for life to appear on it. The race has always won. If it hadn't won, it wouldn't be here. Tonight, and tomorrow night and all the other nights that are to be until the issue is decided, the human race must fight again. Either we survive or the *draal* survives. In this battle there is no compromise."

HE PAUSED. "Only tonight, when I learned what had happened to your father and what had happened to a farmer's cow, did I finally realize that what I had thought was merely a method of becoming wealthy was in reality the bugle call of battle. And I also realized—to my eternal pain—that the bugle call had found me playing the part of traitor to my own kind."

For the first time he forgot to whisper. The words rang clear and compelling in the silent room.

"I hope," Featherstone continued. "I fervently hope that the historians of the future—if there are any—will write that only through ignorance of the true nature of the enemy did I play the part of a traitor. I know, however, that ignorance is no excuse. In the battle of evolution, in the battle to determine which species survives and which dies, only results count. You either survive or die, and ignorance is not an excuse for dying but a reason for it. I know this. I hope, however, that the historians will write that the ignorant traitor was at least sorry."

Graham felt the struggle going on in the man's soul. Featherstone had been false to the oldest loyalty of the race, the loyalty to ones own kind. He was paying part of the price in bitterness. Graham wondered how he would pay the whole price. For always the whole price is exacted for disloyalty. And the price is never merely a single pound of flesh.

"The *draal* tricked me," Featherstone continued. "I thought I could use it. All the time it was using me. It taught me how to create the *dreth,* how to blend and mold and feed the forces that go into that hideous little monstrosity—"

"*Dreth?*" Graham questioned.

"I forgot you didn't know. The thing that killed the dog. That was a *dreth*. The things you saw down in the building below us, those were *dreth*. If you ask me what they are, I can only tell you that they are fields of electro-magnetic force. As to the powers they possess, I can only say I don't know, but I suspect their ability to kill by turning flesh into bone is merely a demonstration of a minor ability. They go through glass as if it didn't exist, they can go through steel, through copper, through any metal that is not several inches thick. Thickness stops them. They can't go through a brick or a stone wall. Too thick. But they can go through the wall of a frame house or a wooden box without even slowing down. They move at a speed of hundreds-possibly thousands—of miles per hour. They may be alive. I don't know about that. They are under the control of the *draal,* which sends them out and calls them back at will. Although they do not possess sight as we know sight, they are most certainly aware of everything around them. They are the things I was using in New York to scare money out of millionaires."

"You said the *draal* controls them," Graham pointed out. "Yet in your studio in New York, you seemed to control one of them."

"Wrong. My control was not direct. It was through the *draal*. In other words, I told the *draal* what I wanted done—choosing always something that the *dreth* could do—and the *draal* sent the *dreth* to do the job. At no time did I have direct control over the *dreth*."

"How did you tell the *draal* what you wanted done?"

"Telepathy," Featherstone answered.

"Telepathy?" Graham echoed.

"Certainly. Direct contact between minds. Oh, don't misunderstand me. I have no telepathic powers. It wasn't my mind, nor was it the power of my mind that made the trick work. The *draal* has the telepathic powers, not me. It reached my mind, learned what I wanted, sent the *dreth* to do the job. The *draal*, in other words, can reach and read my mind. For the love of heaven, Graham, why do you think I've been talking in a whisper, why do you think I've been jumping every time the wind blows that curtain, why do you think I'm so blasted scared? Because the *draal* can read my mind!

"All the time I've been talking to you, Graham, I've been afraid the *draal* was reading my mind. I'm scared to death that it knows what I have been saying and what I have been thinking. If it has been reading my mind—if it knows that I realize how dangerous it is and what a horrible menace it is not only to us but to the whole human race—then at any second a *dreth* may whistle through the walls of this room and kill all of us!"

The wind tugged at the curtain as Featherstone stopped speaking. Every sense tense with expectancy, he stared at the moving cloth. There was silence in the room, the sort of silence that comes from dreadful expectancy.

"WHEN I first found the *draal*, my own greed obscured my vision," Featherstone said. "I was so intrigued with how I could turn the discovery to my own advantage—how I could use the *draal* to make myself rich that I did not realize it was using me. When it told me how to make a *dreth*, I was delighted. I could use the *dreth* to clean up. Only when the second *dreth* appeared out of the same crucible of force in which the first one was created, did I begin to become suspicious. One *dreth* was all right. I could use one of them. Two of them, however, I did not need. Then there were three, then four, then five of them. My suspicions grew stronger. When I learned of the death of Mr. Chambers, my suspicions became certainties. The *draal* was using me."

His whispering voice faded into silence and Graham got a glimpse of the grim drama that had been played here in this hillside house. Featherstone had tried to use the *draal,* but he had been used instead!

"The *draal* itself is almost helpless," Featherstone continued. "It can barely move. Possibly, at one time, it possessed full, free-ranging, unlimited motive powers, but in the centuries during which it was buried in the ground, it lost almost all of its ability to move. Having no hands, it can't use tools. A man without legs or arms would be in much the same position as the *draal.* Such a man could not move, nor could he use tools to make himself a pair of artificial legs or a gun to defend himself. He might have the most brilliant and powerful mind of any individual in the human race but the only way he could use his mind would be to tell someone else what to do and how to do it."

He paused. Off in the night a whippoorwill was calling.

"The *draal* used me as its legs and arms," he continued. "It used me as its tool. I brought to it the equipment it needed. And it flattered me, oh so subtly it flattered me! It told me what a smart person I was, how intelligent I was, and how the *dreth* would aid me. I never did realize that its real purpose was to get a *dreth* created, that once a *dreth* was created the *draal* was probably the most powerful entity on this planet!"

He looked at Graham. "Now you understand why I said I have played the part of a traitor to my own kind. I have brought into existence a monster the like of which the human race has never seen. Because of me the bugle call of battle is blowing tonight all over the world. Graham—" His clenched fist smacked into his open palm in a sound as loud in that stillness as a pistol shot. "Graham, we either destroy the *draal,* or destroy the *dreth* and thus take away all powers from it, or there is in motion a force that will either conquer or destroy the human race. It's either or else, Graham. Either or else."

"What do you propose to do?" Graham said slowly. "How are you going to destroy the *draal*, how are you going to render it powerless?"

"That's what I don't know," Featherstone answered. "Oh, I know how to destroy it, or at least I think I know how. Actually the plastic ball in which it is encased seems fragile. A single quick blow from a hammer ought to smash it. The question is, how to hit that single blow and stay alive! If you try to strike it, it will read your mind, and you will be dead before you can pick up a hammer."

HE BEGAN to pace the floor again.

As he walked, he talked to himself. "It's got to be done right away. Tonight. There are five of the *dreth* now. Tomorrow there may be ten. Every new *dreth* is a new weapon. So it's got to be done now. And I'm the man who has got to do it."

Featherstone shuddered away from that decision. He didn't want to decide that he was the man who had to destroy the *draal*. He didn't want to take that chance. He wanted to stay alive as much as any man. The loyalty to his kind, the loyalty to his own people, was driving him. He took a deep breath, stopped pacing.

"I'll go do it," he said.

"And I'll go with you," Graham said.

Featherstone stared at him in blank astonishment. "You will not!" he said.

"This is my fight too," Graham argued, "You may need help, and need it badly."

"I'm not thinking about that," Featherstone answered. "You are a stranger to the *draal*. The instant you step inside that building it will begin probing into your mind. It will sense your intentions in a second. No, Graham, you're not going with me."

The ghost of a smile showed on the lean face. "Though I thank you for your good intentions."

"What about it reading *your* mind?" Graham retorted.

"It knows me. It has accepted me. Unless I do something to arouse its suspicions, it will pay no attention to me. Louie, where are you going?"

The little scar-faced man had started to sneak from the room.

"I—I was just—just going to step aside for a breath of fresh air," He answered. His face was gray with sudden fear.

"You were going to take a run-out powder on me," Featherstone accused. "But you're not going to get away with it. You are going to help me carry the last load of stuff down to that building."

"No!" Louie whispered. "Not down there. Not when you're going to try—"

"You've been helping all evening," Featherstone answered. "You've been in and out of that building a dozen times tonight. The *draal* knows you. You'll be safe enough."

Suddenly Featherstone's face turned grim.

"Supposing I fail?" He grunted, pondering his words for a few moments. Then he looked toward his frightened assistant. "Come on, Louie. I won't fail...I *can't* fail. Get a hold of the other end of this box."

Louie started to speak, but Featherstone cut him off in mid-sentence.

"No Louie, there is no use in trying to argue. You've been with me all evening. If you don't make this trip with me, your absence might arouse the suspicions of the *draal.*"

Each man carrying one end of a heavy packing box, they went out the door and into the darkness. Beads of sudden sweat were visible on the face of the little man, but

Featherstone, on the contrary, showed no sign of fear. His face—calm and composed—was lit by an inner glow.

Graham watched them walk through the door. He took a deep breath. "There goes destiny," he said.

CHAPTER EIGHT

MILDRED Chambers stayed very close to Graham, as close as she could get. "I'm scared to death," she whispered. "I've never been so frightened in all my life."

Graham could feel her trembling. "So am I," he answered. "And Baby, we've got reason to be."

"Do—do you believe that story he told?"

"Do I believe it?" Graham gasped. "Good lord! Do you think Featherstone was lying?"

"No—it isn't that, I think he was telling the truth, or what he thought was the truth. But the—well, the brain, the *draal*—that seems so weird, so incredible—"

"Haven't you yet discovered that this is a weird world?" Graham interrupted. "There isn't a fact in any physics textbook, a theorem in any geometry, a statement in any history that isn't downright weird when you stop and think about it. Yes, the *draal* is weird. So is the brain of a man, so is the brain of a dog, so is the brain of an earth worm."

Graham talked jerkily. His words came from the top part of his mind. The rest of his mind was concentrated on what was happening in the building at the foot of the hill. Would Featherstone succeed?

Mildred Chambers sensed and voiced his thoughts.

"Do you think he will be able—to smash it?" she whispered.

"He's got to smash it!" Graham answered fiercely. "And how I hate the thought of that!"

"What?" the girl gasped in surprise. "You mean you don't want him to succeed?"

"It isn't that," Graham answered. "He's got to succeed. It's—do you realize that this is the first time in human history when a man has had a chance to talk to a reasoning creature other than his own kind? The stories the *draal* could tell! Its origin, its history, where it came from—these things would be tremendously interesting and valuable to us. I hate to have to destroy the source of so much information. That's what I mean. The *draal* unquestionably has to be destroyed, if the human race is to continue its existence. Yet I hate to destroy something that could do so much for us. I think Featherstone feels the same way I do. Both of us know that the *draal* is like a stolen million-dollar bill. It's worth a mint to you, but if you try to spend it, you'll get thrown in jail for the rest of your life."

The wind tugged at the curtain. Footsteps sounded on the path outside. The door opened. Louie entered.

"What happened?" Graham demanded.

The little man was trembling. He wiped sweat from his face, tried to think what happened.

"He sent me back," Louie said. "We took the box inside the building and he said I could come back up here. I think he was afraid I might reveal too much."

"Has he smashed it?"

"Not when I left, he hadn't." Louie remembered the other things that had happened.

There's only one *dreth* down there," he said.

"Eh?"

"And there's a dead man just outside the building!"

"A dead man?"

"Yes. A state trooper."

"A state trooper? Where did he come from?"

"I don't know," Louie answered. "There's one other thing—" He frowned, tried to think. "Oh, yes. I remember now. There are lights in the sky."

"What?"

"If you step outside, you can see them."

THE LIGHTS weren't in the sky. They were down on the horizon and were reflected against the sky. There were two small glows to the east and toward the north there was a bigger one. At the nearer glow, tiny tips of flame could be seen reaching up into the night.

"Fires," Graham said. "I'm guessing, but I think those two smaller glows are houses on fire. The bigger one—"

He paused as a sudden thought popped into his mind. "Louie, where's Elm Point? What direction is it from here?"

The little man's finger pointed in the direction of the biggest glow of light. "It's right about there," he said.

"That's what I was afraid of," Graham answered.

"What do you think it is?" Mildred Chambers asked.

"I think it isn't any more," Graham answered. "I think it's burning down. I think the whole town is on fire. And I think the glow nearest to us is coming from the burning house of a farmer named Wakely."

"Oh."

Graham was silent. He could smell smoke now. Smoke in the drifting wind. The odor was dim but it was certainly the smell of smoke.

"Did you say there was only one *dreth* down there now?" Graham asked.

There was no answer. Graham looked quickly around. Louie was gone.

"I don't blame him," Graham said. And I think—" He looked at the girl. "How did you get here?"

"Where did—what did you say?"

"How did you get here?"

"In my car."

"Where is it?"

"Parked up there on the side of the road."

"I think you had better go to your car and use it to get the hell away from here. Come on. I'll take you up to it."

He took her by the arm, gently pushed her toward the road. When she protested, he didn't insist.

"You may be right at that," he said.

"It may not be exactly easy to get away from here."

He wasn't paying much attention to what he was saying. He was watching a new glow of light that was coming into sight off to the left and a mile or two away.

Off there in the darkness another farmer's house and barn were going up in flames.

The night was peaceful, calm, serene. The moon shone placidly over the rounded hills. There was no hint of danger, no suggestion that anything was wrong except the fires that were throwing their glow on the dark curtain of the night.

Down below them a rectangle of intensely violet light suddenly appeared as a door opened in the squat building that had been erected there. Featherstone came out of the building.

They heard him close the door. They heard him coming up the path toward them. As he walked up the path in the smoky darkness, they could hear him giggling. He saw them standing in the path, stopped and stared at them, then giggled again.

"It was waiting for me," he said. "All the time I was talking to you, it was reading my mind. When I went inside the building it was waiting for me and it had a *dreth* all ready for action."

He giggled again.

GRAHAM took one step forward.

Smack! His open hand struck Featherstone's face.

"Damn you!" Featherstone snarled. "Damn you, Graham. Who the hell do you think you are?"

Graham stepped back. "You were giggling," he said.

"I was—what? Oh." Wonder was in Featherstone's voice. "Oh I see. Thanks. Or maybe I shouldn't thank you. Maybe it would have been better to go crazy."

"What happened?" Graham said.

"What happened? Oh…a cop is what happened. A state trooper no less. I don't know where in the hell he came from or why he turned up here, but while we were talking, he was snooping around. He tried to go into that building. That's all, brother, that's all. We've got a dead cop on our hands."

"So Louie said."

"So Louie told you about him, did he? Well, did he tell you the rest of it?"

"No."

"The rest of it—" Featherstone sounded like he was about to start giggling again. "The *draal* thought the cop was trying to attack it. I don't know what that cop was thinking while he was snooping around but the *draal* certainly thought he was dangerous. He scared the *draal*. The *draal* not only killed him, but it decided to clear out all humans within a ten-mile radius. It would be safer, the *draal* decided. It's clearing them out now."

Featherstone nodded toward the circle of fires on the skyline. While he was talking, another one had popped into sight.

"Compared to what's happening around here right now, hell's fire and brimstone raining from the sky would be like a summer shower. Hell's out for noon, Graham, hell's out for noon for sure."

In the darkness the night wind was tangy with the pungent odor of smoke.

Featherstone looked at Graham.

"The *draal* wants to talk to you," he said. "To both of you. Yes, it knows you're here. It sent me to tell you to come down and talk about it."

"In that case," Graham answered. "I guess we had better go talk to it."

"I guess you had," Featherstone said. "If you want to stay alive."

As they went down the path together, Featherstone started giggling again.

"It says it can use us," he said. "It says that's the reason we're still alive."

Featherstone led the way into the building. Graham followed him. Mildred Chambers entered last. This was one situation where ladies did not go first.

The big room was bright with violet light.

THE *draal* lay in a cup-like receptacle. Around it and under it was some sort of a complicated electrical machine. Relays were clicking softly in the machine, transformers were humming. A maze of wires ran from the relays to the cup in which the *draal* lay. Through the wires it controlled the operations of the machine.

Graham could not guess the purpose of the machine.

As he entered the room, he was aware something had suddenly entered his mind and he knew that the *draal* was probing through the channels of his brain as it read his thoughts.

"That is close enough," a voice whispered in his mind.

Ten feet away from the machine, it stopped them. It would not let them come closer.

Above the machine, darting about like a huge bee in the sunlight, moving too rapidly for the eye to follow, was a *dreth*.

On guard!

Like three slaves, they stood in a row facing the *draal.*

It read their minds.

Graham knew that he was being weighed and measured as a potential antagonist. How dangerous was he? How dangerous was the girl? The *draal* wanted to use them as tools but it also wanted to know how dangerous were the tools it proposed to use.

It would have preferred to kill them outright, to destroy them. That would have been safest. But for some reason it needed them, had to use them, and it could not kill them until its need for them was finished.

It was evaluating them as potential danger spots.

Graham rigidly excluded such thinking from his conscious mind he did not want the *draal* to know he knew what it was doing—but far under the surface of his mind he knew why the *draal* was studying them so carefully.

It had to use dangerous tools. And it was afraid of them. Therefore in some way they did not know about, they menaced its safety. It had a weak spot.

Then it spoke.

"There is work to be done," a voice whispered in Graham's mind. "You must do that work. If you do it well, you will be well rewarded."

There was a strong hypnotic quality in the voice that whispered through his mind, a seductive, luring quality. It urged him to do what the brain wanted done, then it talked about the reward that would be his.

That reward was knowledge. If he helped the *draal,* it would give him knowledge, it would lift aside the veil that curtained the truth, would help him learn some of the things he had always wanted to know.

In the rigidly partitioned-off part of his mind that he was keeping from thinking, he knew the *draal* had discovered the outstanding facet of his character—the urge to know—and had shrewdly taken advantage of it in offering him his reward for service.

He shook his head.

"No," he said.

Featherstone looked quickly at him.

"Have you gone mad?" Featherstone demanded.

"Probably," Graham answered. "But sane or mad, I will not aid the thing in that machine until I know what I am doing."

"Ah!" the *draal* said.

The *dreth* moved toward Graham.

"No!" Featherstone shouted. "He doesn't know what he's saying. He will do the work that must be done."

"I know he will," the *draal's* mental whisper came. "But first he needs a lesson."

Out from the swiftly moving *dreth* a flash of almost invisible light puffed. It struck Graham.

Mildred Chambers screamed. Featherstone looked appalled.

Pain—red, raging, dripping pain tore Graham's body apart.

Suddenly he knew why the little dog in the steel box in Featherstone's studio had howled in great pain. The same thing that had happened to the dog was now happening to him.

He was being turned into bone. He couldn't move a muscle in his body.

Pain struck every nerve ending in his body.

He tried to scream and his lungs wouldn't work.

Abruptly the flashing light was gone from the *dreth*.

The pain relaxed its numbing hold and Graham could breath again.

"You can do the work I want done, or you can have more of this," the *draal* whispered in his mind. "Take your choice."

"I'll work," Graham faltered.

He knew he had no choice.

"Then get busy," the *draal* said.

It told them what was to be done.

CHAPTER NINE

THE VOICE of the announcer coming over the radio was almost hysterical.

"An entire community in the northern part of New York State was wiped out last night by fires of mysterious origin," the announcer said. "Fragmentary reports, far from complete as yet, indicate the death toll may run into thousands. The pilot of an observation plane, which flew over the area early this morning, reported that the small town of Elm Point has been completely destroyed and that hundreds of fires are still smoldering in and around the town. According to this same report, every farmhouse and barn in the vicinity of Elm Point is a pile of blackened ashes. There has been no communication with Elm Point since late last night.

"Scientists who had been called in can advance no suggestion as to the cause of the catastrophe, but hints from other sources indicate that possibly some type of atomic reaction has taken place in this area.

"Exploring parties are carefully approaching the town of Elm Point. Units of the National Guard have been mobilized. And the question has been asked: Has the United States been attacked? Is this war?

"If this is war, what nation is attacking this country?

"Further reports will follow as soon as they are received in this studio. Keep tuned to this station for the news."

The voice of the announcer went into silence.

Graham tiredly shut off the radio.

There was reason for his being tired. He had worked all night long.

It was noon before the *draal* permitted them to stop for a minute. Then it allowed them to leave the big building at the foot of the hill and to come up to the house and prepare food for themselves. After that, they could rest for three hours.

Then back to work.

The *draal* realized they needed food and rest if they were to continue working.

It had no intention of killing them before they had finished constructing the odd piece of electrical equipment they were working so hard to assemble.

They were its hands, its tools. As such, they were valuable to it.

When they left the building at the foot of the hill and came up to the house to prepare food, a *dreth* came with them.

Never still for an instant, it darted around the room above their heads, always watching them.

The eyes of the girl tried to follow the *dreth* as it darted around the room. Fatigue and fear had drained all color out of her face. She had worked side by side with the two men. The *draal* had not spared her because she was a woman.

"What are we going to do?" she whispered.

"What can we do?" Featherstone answered. "That damned thing can read our minds. No matter what we try to do, it will know what we are planning before we do it."

"I think I can tell when it's trying to read my mind," Graham said. "I get little darting pains high up in my forehead every time it starts probing into my brain."

FEATHERSTONE looked up quickly. "Then you've got something," he said. "I've never been able to tell when it was reading my mind and when it wasn't. If you can tell when it's reading your mind, then you know when it's safe for you to think. Maybe—maybe you can think of something to do."

"That's the catch," Graham wryly answered. "I know when it's safe to think but I can't think of anything, I just don't know enough. There's a weakness somewhere. I know that much. I suspect the weakness has something to do with that piece of machinery we're putting together. But I don't know what it is."

"Think, man!" Featherstone urged. "And keep any discoveries you make to yourself. Don't try to tell me anything you find out. The *draal* might find them out by reading my mind."

A flash of fire showed on Featherstone's lean face as he spoke.

Like Graham and the girl, Featherstone was desperately tired and almost beyond hope. Graham's words brought a spark of life back to him.

To fight the *draal*, they needed to mow much more about it than they knew. Its strength, its weaknesses, if any, how it worked, what it was trying to do—they needed to know these things. Not knowing them, they were like sleepwalkers in the dark. Any misstep might lead to destruction. And they didn't know when they were taking a misstep because they didn't know what was right and what was wrong. If they made a move that definitely threatened the *draal*, the result would be swift and exceedingly painful death.

That didn't matter. All three of them were long past the point of thinking about themselves. What did matter was that the *draal* must not be permitted to consolidate its position, it must not be permitted to increase its strength.

There was only room on the planet for one ruling race.

"I want to know what that machine is we're being forced to build," Graham said. "I think the clue to the weakness of the *draal* is in that machine—"

Little prickles of pain squirmed through his brain as he spoke.

He quickly forced himself to think about something else. He tried to watch the *dreth* circling over their heads. He let horror of that weird little monstrosity flood through his mind.

The *draal* was trying to read his mind.

It was on guard. It was watchful. It was alert.

Graham ignored the little darting pains high up behind his forehead. Eventually they went away. He dared to breathe again.

Two hours later the *dreth* herded them back down the hill to the building where the *draal* waited.

"Back to work!" the order flowed into their minds. "Back to work."

There was insistence in the whisper in their minds. The *draal* wanted them to hurry. It wanted them to finish the job it was making them do. That job was important. They must work as fast as they could.

Graham glanced over at the cup-like receptacle where the crystal ball with the central core of blackness rested. He could see little glimmering lights moving in that core of blackness and he knew that the *draal* was watching him.

Darting pains moved behind his forehead.

"Work," the *draal* said, in his mind. "The new energy source—"

The thinking blanked out.

Graham's face showed nothing. He kept his mind under rigid control. But he then knew what they were building.

IT WAS a generator, an electrical generator. Unlike any dynamo ever built on Earth, it worked on some new and unknown principle, but it was unquestionably an electrical generator. The cables they had already installed and connected to a heavy switch that fed into the power lines that came into the building. The switch was open. Graham had assumed that when the switch was closed, current would flow from the power lines to the machine they were assembling. He saw now that the reverse was true. When the switch was closed, current would flow from the generator to the intricate piece of electrical machinery that served as a support for the crystal ball that was the *draal*.

"Power," he thought. "We're building a new source of power for it. It needs this new power source desperately. I wonder why?"

The *draal* was getting the power it used from the high line that had been extended to his building. The faint hum of the transformer on the poles outside was audible inside the big room.

Plenty of power was coming in over that high line.

Why did the *draal* need a new source of power?

The racing motor of a fighter-bomber tore a hole in the air as the ship passed less than a hundred feet above the roof of the building.

Boom!

The building rocked on its foundations.

Graham picked himself up off the floor. Featherstone and Mildred Chambers looked dazedly up at him. The explosion had thrown them to the floor also.

"What—what was that?" the girl whispered.

"That," said Graham indifferently, "was a bomb. Probably a five hundred pounder—"

As though nothing had happened, he started back to work on the machine they were assembling.

"A bomb?" the girl questioned.

"Yes," Graham answered. "Hand me that screwdriver, will you? One of these screws has stripped its threads and must be removed."

He kept his face expressionless; he kept all thoughts of exultation out on his mind. Prickles of pain behind his forehead warned him not to do any thinking.

Subconsciously he knew what had happened. That was an army plane that had passed overhead, a fighter-bomber. It had dropped a bomb aimed at this building.

Somebody outside, somebody in authority, knew what was happening. Somebody knew that the source of the mysterious fires that had destroyed Elm Point and the surrounding community had their source in this building. Fighter-bombers were moving up. There were certainly armored cars back there on the road—possibly even tanks. The country had armored cars and tanks to burn.

The appearance of the plane meant one thing: Louie had escaped. The little man in the baggy clothes, the little man who had been so scared, had gotten to someone in authority and told his story.

Deep in his mind Graham wondered how Louie had ever managed to convince a public official that he was telling the truth. Louie's story must have sounded utterly fantastic. But he had convinced somebody that it was the truth. Of course, Louie had the evidence of a destroyed town and innumerable burned farmhouses to back him up. That must have helped immeasurably. At any rate, he had certainly told his story. He had convinced somebody that something housed in the building must be destroyed no matter what the cost.

A fighter-bomber had been sent to do the job, but its first bomb had missed. The plane's motor roared somewhere off in the sky as it made a turn and started back to drop a second bomb.

"They're aiming at us," Featherstone said.

"Oh, no," Graham answered, "nothing like that."

FEATHERSTONE'S face was a study in mixed emotions. He knew he was a target for the next bomb. He knew, also, that something else was also the target. He knew he couldn't run.

The *draal* wouldn't let him run. The *dreth* would kill him if he tried to run.

All he could do was wait.

In that moment, greatness showed in Featherstone. He managed to grin, then went back to work.

He completely ignored the racing motor in the sky.

Graham desperately controlled his mind.

The *draal* was trying to find out what was happening. The explosion of that bomb had certainly jarred it.

It suspected and probably knew it was being attacked.

But it didn't know what was attacking it, or how the attack was coming.

If they knew very little about it, it in turn knew very little about them. The great outside world, the world of cities and nations, the world of men and machines, of fighting men and fighting machines, it knew little or nothing about this world.

It didn't even know there were such things as fighter-bombers.

All it knew was that something had roared through the sky and then there had been an explosion.

It was trying to find out what was happening. It was trying to get information on that roar in the sky and that shattering explosion from the minds of the humans in the room.

They closed their minds.

They told it nothing.

The howl of the motor was growing louder.

The plane was circling preparatory to making another run on its target. This time the pilot would not miss his aim.

Acting as if nothing whatsoever was happening, the three humans worked calmly on the generator they were fitting together. Featherstone rose to his feet and went to one of the packing boxes for another part. Acting on instructions from the *draal*, he had ordered these parts from a large electrical supply house. Now he was quietly helping fit them together.

So far as his face showed or his mind revealed, there were no such things as airplanes and bombs on earth.

MILDRED CHAMBERS incautiously dropped a heavy housing on a finger. She swore and put the mashed digit in her mouth.

She had never heard of such a thing as a five hundred-pound bomb.

Graham removed the screw with stripped threads from its seat.

Far up in the sky, he heard the plane start its dive toward them.

The pilot of that plane was incautious. Nobody was shooting at him. He didn't think there was any danger. He shoved the nose of his ship down toward his target.

Graham felt the pains abruptly vanish from his forehead.

The *draal* had ceased trying to read his mind. It has stopped trying to find out what was happening from him.

It had sought other sources for the information it needed.

The motor of the diving plane was overhead.

Thunder exploded in the sky.

Wincing, Graham listened. At that moment, he would have given his life for the sound of a diving motor.

He heard no such sound.

There was no such sound in the sky.

There wasn't even an airplane in the sky any more.

There were only bits of shattered metal and fragments of flesh plunging down to earth.

A *dreth,* on guard somewhere overhead, had been sent to meet the plane.

The plane had exploded.

There was silence in the big room. Under the cup-like depression where the *draal* rested, relays clicked furiously. There was no other sound.

Outside there were several thumps as pieces of shattered metal hit the ground.

Featherstone looked like a man who has just heard his death sentence pronounced.

The three humans had automatically stopped working, when they heard the plane explode.

"Back to work!" the voice of the *draal* lashed their minds. "Hurry. Work faster."

As he hastily resumed his interrupted task, Graham heard another sound—the far-off throb of many motors in the sky.

Not one motor this time.

Many motors.

CHAPTER TEN

THE MOTORS in the sky moved closer. There were six or seven planes at least in the flight. Judging by the racket they were making, they were twin-engined bombers.

The *draal* had destroyed a single plane. Would it be able to destroy a flight of bombers?

Graham could hear relays clicking frantically in the electrical equipment housed under the *draal*. Somewhere in the sky overhead he had a vision of *dreths* racing madly in response to those clicking relays. Four of the *dreths* were available to fight the planes. One *dreth* remained in the room with them, constantly on guard. As long as that hideous little monstrosity darted around them like a giant bee, they were helpless.

The motors were as loud as thunder in the sky, gnawing at the air like a giant hound gnawing a bone.

Boom!

Real thunder shook the foundations of the earth.

Graham groaned. He knew what that clap of thunder meant. A *dreth* had either passed through the fuel tanks of a bomber, exploding the gasoline, or it had exploded the bombs in the racks of the plane. Either way, the answer was the same.

A plane exploding in blazing wrath!

Panic hit the flight of bombers. Graham heard the even drone of the motors change as the pilots broke formation.

The pilots didn't know what was happening. One of their ships had exploded. They suspected that some sort of a radar beam was being used against them that blew up their fuel tanks. They didn't know what they were fighting. Their orders were to blow up the group of buildings on the side of the hill. It looked so easy they were suspicious. When one of their ships exploded without apparent cause, panic hit them. They would have rode through a sky full of blasting ack-ack, they would have fought their way through to their objective against fighter opposition, but the mysterious explosion of one of their ships startled them into momentary panic. They broke formation.

And as they started to scatter, another one of their planes exploded.

They couldn't see what was attacking them but they knew now that they were being attacked. The explosion of the first ship might have been an accident, but when two ships exploded, the possibility of accident was ruled out.

The three humans in the laboratory heard the sound of motors die out in the sky.

There was a note of triumph in the rattle of clicking relays under the *draal*.

There seemed, somehow, to be fewer of the relays in operation now. There had been several and the clicking had been almost continuous. Now there seemed to be only two of the little instruments in operation.

Work! the *draal* snarled in their minds.

As they bent again to their task, the spray of violet light at the far end of the room quickened in intensity. Simultaneously the throb of the transformers grew more labored.

More power was being taken from the high line.

"Another *dreth* is being created," Featherstone whispered, in answer to the question on Graham's face. He nodded toward the spray of violet light. "That's where the *dreths* are created."

"Reinforcements?" Graham said.

"Replacements rather than reinforcements," Featherstone said.

"Eh? I don't understand."

"Listen to the relays," Featherstone answered. "Each relay controls a *dreth.*"

GRAHAM HAD already noticed that fewer relays seemed to be in operation. He listened closely. Only two relays were working.

"What happened to the three other *dreths?*" the almost soundless whisper formed on his lips.

"They destroyed the planes and were themselves destroyed in the explosion," Featherstone explained.

"Then there are only two *dreths* left!" Graham said. "The one in here watching us and one somewhere on guard outside. If those planes will only come back now!"

One *dreth* was on guard somewhere outside. Three others had been destroyed. If the bombers would only return, one plane would surely be destroyed, but the others would get through to drop their bombs without molestation.

Graham listened. The sky was quiet. There was no sound in the still air of the late afternoon.

Somewhere off in the distance the planes were no doubt reporting in and asking for further instructions.

Would they be ordered to continue the attack or would they be pulled off?

In war, they would be ordered back to the attack. But the country wasn't officially at war. With two planes already lost, it would be a brave commander who risked further destruction of his ships, further loss of life, until a complete investigation had revealed the necessity for the action.

In the spray of violet light at the far end of the room Graham saw something rise up.

A new *dreth.*

A new balance of blended force and counterforce.

It moved sluggishly in the violet glow. Like a butterfly that has just crawled from its cocoon and is growing wings in the sunlight, the *dreth* drifted uncertainly in the violet light.

The violet light was developing it, giving it strength.

Under the *draal* a new relay began to click slowly.

Working feverishly at the generator they were building, Graham felt like praying.

Whoom!

Something that tore through the air like an express train just missed the roof of the building. It exploded two or three hundred yards away.

It was a shell from a 99-millimeter cannon that was mounted on a tank destroyer.

While the planes had attacked overhead, units of the ground forces had moved into position.

The first shell they fired had missed.

Graham groaned. They would never get to fire another shell. The single *dreth* that remained outside would blow the tank destroyer to bits and before another attack could be launched, the new *dreth* growing stronger by the second in the violet spray would be ready for action.

He looked at the *dreth* in the violet light to see how far advanced it was.

The light was gone.

The violet spray was not flooding upward.

He was suddenly aware that two sounds that had been always present in the laboratory were now missing. The clicking of the relays and the labored hum of the transformers drawing current from the high line.

These sounds were still.

The transformer was silent.

The relays were still.

Something, drifting like a falling leaf, was floating to the floor before his eyes.

He needed seconds to realize what it was.

Then he recognized it.

It was the *dreth* that had been guarding them.

Powerless, it floated downward.

"The power is off!" Graham heard himself shouting. "The power is off."

He was already on his feet and racing toward the crucible that held the crystal ball that was the *draal*.

"Stay away! Stay away from me! I'll turn the *dreth* on you!" Weak thought impulses chattered in his mind.

The *draal* sounded like a frightened monkey seeing death approach.

Graham and Featherstone were both darting toward it. Both had realized what had happened. Graham got there first. He jerked the *draal* out of the receptacle where it rested. Simultaneously he turned and shouted at Mildred Chambers.

"Get outside and wave a white flag. Wave anything but get outside before that tank destroyer takes a second shot at us."

She staggered rather than ran to the door. They could hear her screaming outside.

The second shot didn't come.

GRAHAM HELD the crystal ball in both hands. Weak impulses, generated by the tiny store of energy the *draal* maintained inside itself, whispered in his brain. The *draal* promised rewards if he would help it. It promised him anything he wanted—wealth, power, knowledge.

He laughed.

"Smash it!" Featherstone urged, trying to snatch the crystal ball away from him.

He shoved Featherstone away. "Smash this?" Graham questioned. "Not until it keeps the promise it made me."

"It's dangerous," Featherstone urged.

"I know it's dangerous but I also know how to control it, now. No, we won't smash it, Swami. We'll just keep it from gaining access to any source of power until we learn everything it knows. We know its secret, Swami, we knew it the instant that shell smashed the high line leading into this building. It's got to have power to operate, power to send forth the *dreths*, power to create them, power to control them. Without power, it's helpless. That's what it was making us build, Swami, a generator to supply power for it. It knew the high line might be broken or the power might be turned off. If that happened, it had to have a source of power that would not fail. That was why it was in such a desperate hurry to get us to finish that generator. Power! It had to have electrical energy, plenty of it. Without that, it's helpless. We'll keep it from getting power until we find out its real history. Think of that, Featherstone…think of it!"

Graham was a little hysterical. All his life he had sought to push aside, if only for a little while, the veil over the face of truth. Now he had in his hands a creature that possessed knowledge beyond that of all humanity. True, the creature was dangerous, it was deadly, but it could be guarded, and Graham had no intention of destroying it until he learned what it knew.

When the men of the guard came cautiously forward in response to the girl waving a tiny pocket-handkerchief, they found two men guarding very, very carefully what looked like a most unusual crystal ball, which—in the confusion that followed—the men managed to leave with.

They're still guarding that crystal ball, these two men and one woman, guarding it to this very day—guarding it with their lives.

The whole story of the unusual events in and around the town of Elm Point has long since died out in the newspapers. The public has forgotten what happened there.

But two men and one woman have not forgotten. They live in an older house on a quiet side street in New York City, an older house that has a high stone wall around it to keep out intruders.

In one of the rooms in that old house is a large safe constructed of a special grade of beryl steel so tough that even a torch would not cut it. The combination to that safe is known to only three people on Earth.

Within that safe is kept a crystal ball. Daily they take the ball from its resting-place and daily they force it to reveal to them more and more of its history. And what a strange history it is.

And some day they hope to learn from it a little of how the universe is constructed.

THE END

If you've enjoyed this book, you will not want to miss these terrific titles…

ARMCHAIR SCI-FI & HORROR DOUBLE NOVELS, $12.95 each

D-31 **A HOAX IN TIME** by Keith Laumer
       INSIDE EARTH by Poul Anderson

D-32 **TERROR STATION** by Dwight V. Swain
       THE WEAPON FROM ETERNITY by Dwight V. Swain

D-33 **THE SHIP FROM INFINITY** by Edmond Hamilton
       TAKEOFF by C. M. Kornbluth

D-34 **THE METAL DOOM** by David H. Keller
       TWELVE TIMES ZERO by Howard Browne

D-35 **HUNTERS OUT OF SPACE** by Joseph Kelleam
       INVASION FROM THE DEEP by Paul W. Fairman,

D-36 **THE BEES OF DEATH** by Robert Moore Williams
       A PLAGUE OF PYTHONS by Frederik Pohl

D-37 **THE LORDS OF QUARMALL** by Fritz Leiber and Harry Fischer
       BEACON TO ELSEWHERE by James H. Schmitz

D-38 **BEYOND PLUTO** by John S. Campbell
       ARTERY OF FIRE by Thomas N. Scortia

D-39 **SPECIAL DELIVERY** by Kris Neville
       NO TIME FOR TOFFEE by Charles F. Meyers

D-40 **RECALLED TO LIFE** by Robert Silverberg
       JUNGLE IN THE SKY by Milton Lesser

ARMCHAIR SCIENCE FICTION CLASSICS, $12.95 each

C-10 **MARS IS MY DESTINATION**
       by Frank Belknap Long

C-11 **SPACE PLAGUE**
       by George O. Smith

C-12 **SO SHALL YE REAP**
       by Rog Phillips

ARMCHAIR SCI-FI & HORROR GEMS SERIES, $12.95 each

G-3 **SCIENCE FICTION GEMS, Vol. Two**
       James Blish and others

G-4 **HORROR GEMS, Vol. Two**
       Joseph Payne Brennan and others

AN APOCALYPSE OF MADNESS

It was on Christmas that the world's freedom died. It was the most extraordinary event in human history. Every man, woman, and child lay in the grip of fear, for no one knew at what moment his nearest friend or casual stranger might suddenly be possessed by some brutal force of mind…and begin to murder and destroy.

For Chandler it was worse than for most. He was both victim and executioner. He had suffered himself, and he had committed a violent crime while under the strange domination. Accused of hoaxing he was driven from his home. He wandered until he found himself in Hawaii and learned that this was the center of the plague—and that he was helpless to do anything about it!

CAST OF CHARACTERS

CHANDLER
He was on trial for rape, but when the foreman read his verdict, it was the beginning of a nightmare far beyond a guilty sentence.

ROSALIE
This former Broadway star was cute, talented, and sexy—and she could snuff out your life at a moment's notice.

KOITSKA
A big, fat out-of-shape Russian—he was one of the terrifying masterminds of the new world order.

HSI
An electronic parts warehouse manager who didn't like talking too much. What was the secret he guarded so closely?

JUDGE ELLITHORP
A death sentence was what he wanted from the jury, even though he had taken an innocent human life himself.

GUY
An unkempt beard covered the pock-marked face of this old codger who was one of the leaders of a weird secret society.

A PLAGUE OF
PYTHONS

By
FREDERIK POHL

ARMCHAIR FICTION
PO Box 4369, Medford, Oregon   97501-0168

CHAPTER ONE

BECAUSE of the crowd, they held Chandler's trial in the all-purpose room of the high school. It smelled of leather and stale sweat. He walked up the three steps to the stage, with the bailiff's hand on his elbow, and took his place at the defendant's table.

Chandler's lawyer looked at him without emotion. He was appointed by the court. He was willing to do his job but his job didn't require him to like his client. All he said was, "Stand up. The judge is coming in."

Chandler got to his feet and leaned on the table while the bailiff chanted his call and the chaplain read some verses from John. He did not listen. The Bible verse came too late to help him, and besides he ached.

When the police arrested him they had not been gentle. There were four of them. They were from the plant's own security force and carried no guns. They didn't need any; Chandler had put up no resistance after the first few moments—that is, he stopped as soon as he could stop—but the police hadn't stopped. He remembered that very clearly. He remembered the nightstick across the side of his head that left his ear squashed and puffy, he remembered the kick in the gut that still made walking painful. He even remembered the series of blows about the skull that had knocked him out.

The bruises along his rib cage and left arm, though, he did not remember getting. Obviously the police had been mad enough to keep right on subduing him after he was already unconscious.

Chandler did not blame them—exactly. He supposed he would have done the same thing.

The judge was having a long mumble with the court stenographer apparently about something that had happened in the Union House the night before. Chandler knew Judge Ellithorp slightly. He did not expect to get a fair trial. The previous December the judge himself, while possessed, had smashed the transmitter of the town's radio station, which he owned, and set fire to the building it occupied. His son-in-law had been killed in the fire.

Laughing, the judge waved the reporter back to his seat and glanced around the courtroom. His gaze touched Chandler lightly, like the flick of the hanging strands of cord that precede a railroad tunnel. The touch carried the same warning: What lay ahead for Chandler was destruction.

"Read the charge," ordered Judge Ellithorp. He spoke very loudly. There were more than six hundred persons in the auditorium; the judge didn't want any of them to miss a word.

The bailiff ordered Chandler to stand and informed him that he was accused of having, on the seventeenth day of June last, committed on the person of Margaret Flershem, a minor, an act of rape— "Louder!" ordered the judge testily.

"Yes, Your Honor," said the bailiff, and inflated his chest. "An Act of Rape under Threat of Bodily Violence," he cried; "and Did Further Commit on the Person of Said Margaret Flershem an Act of Aggravated Assault—"

Chandler rubbed his aching side, looking at the ceiling. He remembered the look in Peggy Flershem's eyes as he forced himself on her. She was only sixteen years old, and at that time he hadn't even known her name.

By FREDERIK POHL

Illustrated by RITTER

PLAGUE OF PYTHONS

The bailiff boomed on: "—and Did Further Commit on that Same Seventeenth Day of June Last on the Person of Ingovar Porter an Act of Assault with Intent to Rape, the Foregoing Being a True Bill Handed Down by the Grand Jury of Sepulpas County in Extraordinary Session Assembled, the Eighteenth Day of June Last."

Judge Ellithorp looked satisfied as the bailiff sat down, quite winded. While the judge hunted through the papers on his desk the crowd in the auditorium stirred and murmured.

A child began to cry.

THE JUDGE stood up and pounded his gavel. "What is it? What's the matter with him? You, Dundon!" The court attendant the judge was looking at hurried over and spoke to the child's mother, then reported to the judge.

"I dunno, Your Honor. All he says is something scared him."

The judge was enraged. "Well, that's just fine! Now we have to take up the time of all these good people, probably for no reason, and hold up the business of this court, just because of a child. Bailiff! I want you to clear this courtroom of all children under—" he hesitated, calculating voting blocks in his head—"all children under the age of six. Dr. Palmer, are you there? Well, you better go ahead with the—prayer." The judge could not make himself say "the exorcism."

"I'm sorry, madam," he added to the mother of the crying two-year-old. "If you have someone to leave the child with, I'll instruct the attendants to save your place for you." She was also a voter.

Dr. Palmer rose, very grave, as he was embarrassed. He glared around the all-purpose room, defying anyone to smile, as he chanted: "Domina Pythonis, I command you, leave! Leave, Hel! Leave, Heloym! Leave, Sother and Thetragrammaton, leave, all unclean ones! I command you! In the name of God, in all of His manifestations!" He sat down again, still very grave. He knew that he did not make nearly as fine a showing as Father Lon, with his resonant *in nomina Jesu Christi et Sancti Ubaldi* and his censer, but the post of exorcist was filled in strict rotation, one month to a denomination, ever since the troubles started. Dr. Palmer was a

Unitarian. Exorcisms had not been in the curriculum at the seminary and he had been forced to invent his own.

Chandler's lawyer tapped him on the shoulder. "Last chance to change your mind," he said.

"No. I'm not guilty, and that's the way I want to plead."

The lawyer shrugged and stood up, waiting for the judge to notice him.

Chandler, for the first time, allowed himself to meet the eyes of the crowd.

He studied the jury first. He knew some of them casually—it was not a big enough town to command a jury of total strangers for any defendant, and Chandler had lived there most of his life. He recognized Pop Matheson, old and stiff, who ran the railroad station cigar stand. Two others were familiar as faces passed in the street. The forewoman, though, was a stranger. She sat there very composed and frowning. All he knew about her was that she wore funny hats. Yesterday's had been red roses when she was selected from the panel; today's was, of all things, a stuffed bird.

He did not think that any of them were possessed. He was not so sure of the audience.

He saw girls he had dated in high school, long before he met Margot; men he worked with at the plant. They all glanced at him, but he was not sure who was looking out through some of those familiar eyes. The visitors reliably watched all large gatherings, at least momentarily; it would be surprising if none of them were here.

"All right, how do you plead," said Judge Ellithorp at last.

Chandler's lawyer straightened up. "Not guilty, Your Honor, by reason of temporary pandemic insanity."

The judge looked pleased. The crowd murmured, but they were pleased too. They had him dead to rights and it would have been a disappointment if Chandler had pleaded guilty. They wanted to see one of the vilest criminals in contemporary human society caught, exposed, convicted and punished; they did not want to miss a step of the process. Already in the playground behind the school three deputies from the sheriff's office were loading their rifles, while the school janitor chalked lines around the handball court to mark where the crowd witnessing the execution would be permitted to stand.

THE PROSECUTION made its case very quickly. Mrs. Porter testified that she worked at McKelvey Bros., the antibiotics plant, where the defendant also worked. Yes, that was him. She had been attracted by the noise from the culture room last—let's see— "Was it the Seventeenth day of June last?" prompted the prosecutor, and Chandler's attorney instinctively gathered his muscles to rise, hesitated, glanced at his client and shrugged. That was right, it was the seventeenth. Incautiously she went right into the room. She should have known better, she admitted. She should have called the plant police right away, but, well, they hadn't had any trouble at the plant, you know, and—well, she didn't. She was a stupid woman, for all that she was rather good-looking, and insatiably curious. She had seen Peggy Flershem on the floor.

"She was all *blood*. And her clothes were—and she was, I mean her—her body was—" With relentless tact the prosecutor allowed her to stammer out her observation that the girl had clearly been raped. And she had seen Chandler laughing and breaking up the place, throwing racks of cultures through the windows, upsetting trays. Of course she had crossed herself and tried a quick exorcism but there was no visible effect; then Chandler had leaped at her. "He was *hateful!* He was just *foul!*" But as he began to attack her, the plant police came, drawn by her screams.

Chandler's attorney did not question.

Peggy Flershem's deposition was introduced without objection from the defense. But she had little to say anyway, having been dazed at first and unconscious later. The plant police testified to having arrested Chandler; a doctor described in chaste medical words the derangements Chandler had worked on Peggy Flershem's virgin anatomy. There was no question from Chandler's lawyer—and, for that matter, nothing to question. Chandler did not hope to pretend that he had not ravished and nearly killed one girl, then done his best to repeat the process on another. Sitting there as the doctor testified, Chandler was able to tally every break and bruise against the memory of what his own body had done. He had been a spectator then, too, as remote from the event as he was now; but that was why they had him on trial. That was what they did not believe.

At twelve-thirty the prosecution rested its case, Judge Ellithorp looking very pleased. He recessed the court for one hour for lunch, and the guards took Chandler back to the detention cell in the basement of the school.

Two Swiss cheese sandwiches and a wax-paper carton of chocolate milk were on the desk. They were Chandler's lunch. As they had been standing, the sandwiches were crusty and the milk lukewarm. He ate them anyway. He knew what the judge looked pleased about. At one-thirty Chandler's lawyer would put him on the stand, and no one would pay very much attention to what he had to say, and the jury would be out at most twenty minutes, and the verdict would be guilty. The judge was pleased because he would be able to pronounce sentence no later than four o'clock, no matter what. They had formed the habit of holding the executions at sundown. As, at that time of year, sundown was after seven, it would all go very well—for everyone but Chandler. For Chandler it would be the end.

CHAPTER TWO

THE ODD thing about Chandler's dilemma was not merely that he was innocent—in a way, that is—but that many who were guilty (in a way; as guilty as he himself, at any rate) were free and honored citizens. Chandler himself was a widower because his own wife had been murdered. He had seen the murderer leaving the scene of the crime, and the man he had seen was in the courtroom today, watching Chandler's own trial. Of the six hundred or so in the court, at least fifty were known to have taken part in one or more provable acts of murder, rape, arson, theft, sodomy, vandalism, assault and battery or a dozen other offenses indictable under the laws of the state. Of course, that could be said of almost any community in the world in those years; Chandler's was not unique. What had put Chandler in the dock was not what his body had been seen to do, but the place in which it had been seen to do it. For everybody knew that medicine and agriculture were never molested by the demons.

Chandler's own lawyer had pointed that out to him the day before the trial. "If it was anywhere but at the McKelvey plant, all right, but there's never been any trouble there. You know that. The trouble with you laymen is you think of lawyers in terms of Perry Mason, right? Rabbit out of the hat stuff. Well, I can't do that. I can only present your case, whatever it is, the best way possible. And the best thing I can do for your case right now is tell you, you haven't got one." At that time the lawyer was still trying to be fair. He was even casting around for some thought he could use to convince himself that his client was innocent, though he had frankly admitted as soon as he introduced himself that he didn't have much hope there.

Chandler protested that he didn't have to commit rape. He'd been a widower for a year, but—

"Wait a minute," said the lawyer. "Listen. You can't make an ordinary claim of possession stick, but what about good old - fashioned insanity?" Chandler looked puzzled, so the lawyer explained. Wasn't it possible that Chandler was—consciously, subconsciously, unconsciously, call it what you will—trying to get revenge for what had happened to his own wife?

No, said Chandler, certainly not! But then he had to stop and think. After all, he had never been possessed before; in fact he had always retained a certain skepticism about "possession"—it seemed like such a convenient way for anyone to do any illicit thing he chose—until the moment when he looked up to see Peggy Flershem walking into the culture room with a tray of agar disks, and was astonished to find himself striking her with the wrench in his hand and ripping at her absurdly floral-printed slacks. Maybe his case was different. Maybe it wasn't the sort of possession that struck at random; maybe he was just off his rocker.

Margot, his wife, had been cut up cruelly. He had seen his friend, Jack Souther, leaving his home hurriedly as he approached; and although he had thought that the stains on his clothes looked queerly like blood, nothing in that prepared him for what he found in the rumpus room. It had taken him some time to identify the spread-out dissection on the floor with his wife Margot... "No," he told his lawyer, "I was shaken up, of course. The worst time was the next night, when there was a knock on the door and I opened it and it was Jack. He'd come to apologize. I—fell apart; but I got over it. I tell you I was possessed, that's all."

"And I tell you that defense will put you right in front of a firing squad," said his lawyer. "And *that's* all."

FIVE OR SIX others had been executed for hoaxing; Chandler was familiar with the ritual. He even understood it, in a way. The world had gone to pot in the previous two years. The real enemy was out of reach; when any citizen might run wild and, when caught, relapse into his own self, terrified and sick, there was a need to strike back. But the enemy was invisible. The hoaxers were only whipping boys—but they were the only targets vengeance had.

The real enemy had struck the entire world in a single night. One day the people of the world went about their business in the gloomy knowledge that they were likely to make mistakes but with, at least, the comfort that the mistakes would be their own. The next day had no such comfort. The next day anyone, anywhere, was likely to find himself seized, possessed, working evil or whimsy without intention and helplessly.

Chandler stood up, kicked the balled-up wax paper from his sandwiches across the floor and swore violently.

He was beginning to wake from the shock that had gripped him. "Damn fool," he said to himself. He had no particular reason. Like the world, he needed a whipping boy too, if only himself. "Damn fool, you know they're going to shoot you!"

He stretched and twisted his body violently, alone in the middle of the room, in silence. He *had* to wake up. He *had* to start thinking. In a quarter of an hour or less the court would reconvene, and from then it was only a steady, quick slide to the grave.

It was better to do anything than to do nothing. He examined the windows of his improvised cell. They were above his head and barred; standing on the table, he could see feet walking outside, in the paved play-yard of the school. He discarded the thought of escaping that way; there was no one to smuggle him a file, and there was no time. He studied the door to the hall. It was not impossible that when the guard opened it he could jump him, knock him out, run...run where? The room had been a storage place for athletic equipment at the end of a hall; the hall led only to the stairs and the stairs emerged into the courtroom. It was quite likely, he thought, that the hall had another flight of stairs somewhere farther along, or through another room. What had he spent his taxes on these years, if not for schools designed with more than one exit in case of fire? But as he had not thought to mark an escape route when he was brought in, it did him no good.

The guard, however, had a gun. Chandler lifted up an edge of the table and tried to shake one of the legs. They did not shake; that part of his taxes had been well enough spent, he thought wryly. The chair? Could he smash the chair to get a club, which would give him a weapon to get the guard's gun?...

Before he reached the chair the door opened and his lawyer came in.

"Sorry I'm late," he said briskly. "Well. As your attorney I have to tell you they've presented a pretty damaging case. As I see it—"

"What case?" Chandler demanded. "I never denied the acts. What else did they prove?"

"Oh, God!" said his lawyer, not quite loudly enough to be insulting. "Do we have to go over that again? Your claim of possession would make a defense if it had happened anywhere else. We know that these cases exist, but we also know that they follow a pattern. Some areas seem to be immune—medical establishments, pharmaceutical plants among them. So they proved that all this happened in a pharmaceutical plant. I advise you to plead guilty."

Chandler sat down on the edge of the table, controlling himself very well, he thought. He only asked: "Would that do me any good at all?"

The lawyer reflected, gazing at the ceiling. "...No. I guess it wouldn't."

Chandler nodded. "So what else shall we talk about? Want to compare notes about where you were and I was the night the President went possessed?"

The lawyer was irritated. He kept his mouth shut for a moment until he thought he could keep from showing it. Outside a vendor was hawking amulets: "St. Ann beads! Witch knots! Fresh garlic, local grown, best in town!" The lawyer shook his head.

"All right," he said, "it's your life. We'll do it your way. Anyway, time's up; Sergeant Grantz will be banging on the door any minute."

He zipped up his briefcase. Chandler did not move. "They don't give us much time anyway," the lawyer added, angry with Chandler and at hoaxers in general but not willing to say so. "Grantz is a stickler for promptness."

Chandler found a crumb of cheese by his hand and absently ate it. The lawyer watched him and glanced at his watch. "Oh, hell," he said, picked up his briefcase and kicked the base of the door. "Grantz! What's the matter with you? You asleep out there?"

CHANDLER was sworn, gave his name, admitted the truth of everything the previous witnesses had said. The faces were still aimed at him, everyone. He could not read them at all any more, could not tell if they were friendly or hating, there were too many and they all had eyes. The jurors sat on their funeral-parlor chairs like cadavers, embalmed and propped, the dead witnessing a wake for the living. Only the forewoman in the funny hat showed signs of life, looking alertly at Chandler, at the judge, at the man next to her, around the auditorium. Maybe it was a good sign. At least she did not have the frozen in concrete, guilty-as-hell look of the others.

His attorney asked him the question he had been waiting for: "Tell us, in your own words, what happened." Chandler opened his mouth, and paused. Curiously, he had forgotten what he wanted to say. He had rehearsed this moment again and again; but all that came out was:

"I didn't do it. I mean; I did the acts, but I was possessed. That's all. Others have done worse, under the same circumstances, and been let off. Just as Fisher was acquitted for murdering the Learnards, as Draper got off after what he did to the Cline boy. As Jack Souther over there was let off after he murdered my own wife. They should be. They couldn't help themselves. Whatever this thing is that takes control, I know it can't be fought. My God, you can't even *try* to fight it!"

He was not getting through.

The faces had not changed. The forewoman of the jury was now searching systematically through her pocketbook, taking each item out and examining it, putting it back and taking out another. But between times she looked at him and at least her expression wasn't hostile. He said, addressing her:

"That's all there is to it. It wasn't me running my body. It was someone else. I swear it before all of you, and before God."

The prosecutor did not bother to question him.

Chandler went back to his seat and sat down and watched the next twenty minutes go by in the wink of an eye, rapid, rapid, they were in a hurry to shoot him. He could hardly believe that Judge Ellithorp could speak so fast, the jurymen rise and file out at a gallop, zip, whisk, and they were back again. Too fast! he cried silently, time had gone into high gear; but he knew that it was only his imagination. The twenty minutes had been a full twelve hundred seconds. And then time, as if to make amends, came to a stop, abrupt, brakes-on. The judge asked the jury for their verdict and it was an eternity before the forewoman arose.

She was beginning to look rather disheveled. Beaming at Chandler—*surely* the woman was rather odd, it couldn't be just his imagination—she fumbled in her pocketbook for the slip of paper with the verdict. But she wore an expression of suppressed laughter.

"I *knew* I had it," she cried triumphantly and waved the slip above her head. "Now, let's see." She held it before her eyes and squinted. "Oh, yes. Judge, we the jury, and so forth and so on—"

She paused to wink at Judge Ellithorp. An uncertain worried murmur welled up in the auditorium. "All that junk, Judge," she explained, "anyway, we unanimously—but *unanimously,* love!—find this son of a bitch innocent. Why," she giggled, "we think he ought to get a medal, you know? I tell you what you do, love, you go right over and give him a big wet kiss and say you're sorry." She kept on talking, but no one heard. The murmur because a mass scream.

"Stop, stop her!" bawled the judge, dropping his glasses. "Bailiff!"

The scream became a word, in many voices chorused:

Possessed!

And beyond doubt the woman was. The men around her hurled themselves away, as from leprosy among them, and then washed back like a lynch mob. She was giggling as they fell on her. "Got a cigarette? No cigarettes in this lousy bag—oh." She screamed as they touched her, went limp and screamed again.

It was a different note this time, pure hysteria: "I couldn't *stop*. Oh, *God.*"

CHANDLER caught his lawyer by the arm and jerked him away from staring at the scene. All of a sudden he was alive again. "You, damn it. Listen! The jury acquitted me, right?"

The lawyer was startled. "Don't be ridiculous. It's a clear case of—"

"Be a lawyer, man! You live on technicalities, don't you? Make this one work for me!"

The attorney gave him a queer, thoughtful look, hesitated, shrugged and got to his feet. He had to shout to be heard. "Your honor! I take it my client is free to go."

He made almost as much of a stir as the sobbing woman, but he out shouted the storm. "The jury's verdict is on record. Granted there was an *apparent* case of possession. Nevertheless—"

Judge Ellithorp yelled back: "No nonsense, you! Listen to me, young man—"

The lawyer snapped, "Permission to approach the bench."

"Granted."

Chandler sat unable to move, watching the brief, stormy conference. It was painful to be coming back to life. It was agony to hope. At least, he thought detachedly, his lawyer was fighting for him; the prosecutor's face was a thundercloud.

The lawyer came back, with the expression of a man who has won a victory he did not expect, and did not want. "Your last chance, Chandler. Change your plea to guilty."

"But—"

"Don't push your luck, boy! The judge has agreed to accept a plea. They'll throw you out of town, of course. But you'll be alive." Chandler hesitated. "Make up your mind! The best I can do otherwise is a mistrial, and that means you'll get convicted by another jury next week."

Chandler said, testing his luck: "You're sure they'll keep their end of the bargain?"

The lawyer shook his head, his expression that of a man who smells something unpleasant. "Your honor! I ask you to discharge the jury. My client wishes to change his plea."

…In the school's chemistry lab, an hour later, Chandler discovered that the lawyer had left out one little detail. Outside there was a sound of motors idling, the police car that would dump him at the town's limits; inside was a thin, hollow hiss. It was the sound of a Bunsen burner, and in its blue flame a crudely shaped iron changed slowly from cherry to orange to glowing straw. It had the shape of a letter "H".

"H" for "hoaxer." The mark they were about to put on his forehead would be with him wherever he went and as long as he lived, which would probably not be long. "H" for "hoaxer," so that a glance would show that he had been convicted of the worst offense of all.

No one spoke to him as the sheriff's man took the iron out of the fire, but three husky policemen held his arms while he screamed.

CHAPTER THREE

THE pain was still burning when Chandler awoke the next day. He wished he had a bandage, but he didn't, and that was that.

He was in a freight car—had hopped it on the run at the yards, daring to sneak back into town long enough for that. He could not hope to hitchhike, with that mark on him. Anyway, hitchhiking was an invitation to trouble.

The railroads were safer—far safer than either cars or air transport, notoriously a lightning rod attracting possession. Chandler was surprised when the train came crashing to a stop, each freight car smashing against the couplings of the one ahead, the engine jolting forward and stopping again.

Then there was silence. It endured.

Chandler, who had been slowly waking after a night of very little sleep, sat up against the wall of the boxcar and wondered what was wrong.

It seemed remiss to start a day without signing the Cross or hearing a few exorcismal verses. It seemed to be mid-morning, time for work to be beginning at the plant. The lab men would be streaming in, their amulets examined at the door. The chaplains would be wandering about, ready to pray a possessing spirit out. Chandler, who kept an open mind, had considerable doubt of the effectiveness of all the amulets and spells—certainly they had not kept him from a brutal rape—but he felt uneasy without them... The train still was not moving. In the silence he could hear the distant huffing of the engine.

He went to the door, supporting himself with one hand on the wooden wall, and looked out. The tracks followed the roll of a river, their bed a few feet higher than an empty three-lane highway, which in turn was a dozen feet about the water. As he looked out the engine brayed twice. The train jolted uncertainly then stopped again.

Then there was a very long time when nothing happened at all.

From Chandler's car he could not see the engine. He was on the convex of the curve, and the other door of the car was sealed. He did not need to see it to know that something was wrong. There should have been a brakeman running with a flare to ward off other trains; but there was not. There should have been a station, or at least a water tank, to account for the stop in the first place. There was not. Something had gone wrong, and Chandler knew what it was. Not the details, but the central fact that lay behind this and behind almost everything that went wrong these days.

The engineer was possessed. It had to be that.

Yet it was odd, he thought, as odd as his own trouble. He had chosen this car with care. It contained eight refrigerator cars full of pharmaceuticals, and if anything was known about the laws governing possession, as his lawyer had told him, it was that such things were almost never interfered with.

Chandler jumped down to the roadbed, slipped on the crushed rock and almost fell. He had forgotten the wound on his forehead. He clutched the sill of the car door, where an ankh and fleur-de-lis had been chalked to ward off demons, until the sudden rush of blood subsided and the pain began to relent. After a moment he walked gingerly to the end of the car, slipped between the cars, dodged the couplers and climbed the ladder to its roof.

It was a warm, bright, silent day. Nothing moved. From his height he could see the Diesel at the front of the train and the caboose at its rear. No people. The train was halted a quarter mile from where the tracks swooped across the river on a suspension bridge. Away from the river, the side of the tracks that had been hidden from him before, was an uneven rock cut and, above it, the slope of a mountain.

By looking carefully he could spot the signs of a number of homes within half a mile or so—the corner of a roof, a glassed-in porch built to command a river view, a twenty-foot television antenna poking through the trees. There was also the curve of a higher road along which the homes were strung.

Chandler took thought. He was alive and free, two gifts more gracious than he had had any right to expect. However, he would need food and he would need at least some sort of bandage for his forehead. He had a wool cap, stolen from the high school, which would hide the mark, though what it would do to the burn on his skin was something else again.

Chandler climbed down the ladder. With considerable pain he gentled the cap over the great raw H on his forehead and began to climb the mountain.

HE KNOCKED on the first door he came to, a great old three-story house with well-tended gardens.

There was a wait. The air smelled warmly of honeysuckle and mown grass, with wild onions chopped down by the blades of the mower. It was pleasant, or would have been in happier times. He knocked again, peremptorily, and the door was opened at once. Evidently someone had been right inside, listening.

A man stared at him. "Stranger, what do you want?" He was short, plump, with an extremely thick and unkempt beard. It did not appear to have been grown for its own sake, for where the facial hair could not be coaxed to grow his skin had the gross pits of old acne.

Chandler said glibly: "Good morning. I'm working my way east. I need something to eat, and I'm willing to work for it."

The man withdrew, leaving the upper half of the Dutch door open. As it looked in on only a vestibule it did not tell Chandler much. There was one curious thing—a lath and cardboard sign, shaped like an arc of a rainbow, lettered:

WELCOME TO ORPHALESE

He puzzled over it and dismissed it. The entrance room, apart from the sign, had a knickknack shelf of Japanese carved ivory and an old-fashioned umbrella rack, but that added nothing to his knowledge. He had already guessed that the owners of this home were well off. Also it had been recently painted; so they were not demoralized, as so much of the world had been demoralized, by the coming of the possessors. Even the elaborate sculpturing of its hedges had been maintained.

The man came back and with him was a girl of fifteen or so. She was tall, slim and rather homely, with a large jaw and an oval face. "Guy, he's not much to look at," she said to the pockmarked man. "Meggie, shall I let him in?" he asked. "Guy, you might as well," she shrugged, staring at Chandler with interest but not sympathy.

"Stranger, come along," said the man named Guy, and led him through a short hall into an enormous living room, a room two stories high with a ten-foot fireplace.

Chandler's first thought was that he had stumbled in upon a wake. The room was neatly laid out in rows of folding chairs, more than half of them occupied. He entered from the side, but all the occupants of the chairs were looking toward him. He returned their stares; he had had a good deal of practice lately in looking back at staring faces, he reflected. "Stranger, go on," said the man who had let him in, nudging him, "and meet the people of Orphalese."

Chandler hardly heard him. He had not expected anything like this. It was a meeting, a Daumier caricature of a Thursday Afternoon Literary Circle, old men with faces like moons, young women with faces like hags. They were strained, haggard and fearful, and a surprising number of them showed some sort of physical defect, a bandaged leg, an arm in a sling or merely the marks of pain on the

features. "Stranger, go in," repeated the man, and it was only then that Chandler noticed the man was holding a pistol, pointed at his head.

CHANDLER sat in the rear of the room, watching. There must be thousands of little colonies like this, he reflected; with the breakdown of long-distance communication the world had been atomized. There was a real fear, well justified, of living in large groups, for they too were lightning rods for possession. The world was stumbling along, but it was lame in all its members; a planetary lobotomy had stolen from it its wisdom and plan. If, he reflected dryly, it had ever had any.

But of course things were better in the old days. The world had seemed on the brink of blowing itself up, but at least it was by its own hand. Then came Christmas.

It had happened at Christmas, and the first sign was on nation-wide television. The old President, balding, grave and plump, was making a special address to the nation, urging good will to men and, please, artificial trees because of the fire danger in the event of H-bomb raids; in the middle of a sentence twenty million viewers had seen him stop, look dazedly around and say, in a breathless mumble, what sounded like: *"Disht dvornyet ilgt."* He had then picked up the Bible on the desk before him and thrown it at the television camera.

The last the televiewers had seen was the fluttering pages of the Book, growing larger as it crashed against the lens, then a flicker and a blinding shot of the studio lights as the cameraman jumped away and the instrument swiveled to stare mindlessly upward. Twenty minutes later the President was dead, as his Secretary of Health and Welfare, hurrying with him back to the White House, calmly took a hand grenade from a Marine guard at the gate and blew the President's party to fragments.

For the President's seizure was only the first and most conspicuous. *"Disht dvornyet ilgt."* C. I. A. specialists were playing the tapes of the broadcast feverishly, electronically cleaning the mumble and stir from the studio away from the words to try to learn, first, the language and second what the devil it meant; but the President who ordered it was dead before the first reel spun, and his successor was not quite sworn in when it became his time to die. The ceremony was interrupted for an emergency call from the War Room, where a very nearly hysterical four-star general was trying to explain why he had ordered the immediate firing of every live missile in his command against Washington, D. C.

Over five hundred missiles were involved. In most of the sites the order was disobeyed, but in six of them, unfortunately, unquestioning discipline won out, thus ending not only the swearing in, the general's weeping explanation, the spinning of tapes, but also some two million lives in the District of Columbia, Maryland, Virginia and (through malfunctioning relays on two missiles) Pennsylvania and Vermont. But it was only the beginning.

THESE were the first cases of possession seen by the world in some five hundred years, since the great casting out of devils of the Middle Ages. A thousand more occurred in the next few days, a hundred in the next hours. The timetable was made up out of scattered reports in the wire service newsrooms, while they still had facilities for spot coverage in any part of the world. (That lasted almost a week.) They identified 237 cases of possession by noon of the next day. Disregarding the dubious items—the Yankee pitcher who leaped from the Manhattan bridge (he had Bright's disease), the warden of San Quentin who seated himself in the gas chamber and, literally, kicked the bucket (did he know the Grand Jury was subpoenaing his books?)—disregarding these, the chronology of major cases that evening was:

8:27 PM, EST: President has attack on television.

8:28 PM, EST: Prime Minister of England orders bombing raid against Israel, alleging secret plot (order not carried out).

8:28 PM, EST: Captain of SSN *Ethan Allen*, surfaced near Montauk Point, orders crash dive and course change, proceeding submerged at flank speed to New York Harbor.

9:10 PM, EST: Eastern Airlines six-engine jet makes wheels up landing on roof of Pentagon, breaking some 1500 windows but causing no other major damage (except to the people aboard the jet); record of this incident fragmentary because entire site charred black in fusion attack two hours later.

9:23 PM, EST: Rosalie Pan, musical-comedy star, jumps off stage, runs up center aisle and vanishes in cab, wearing beaded bra, G-string and $2500 headdress. Her movements are traced to Newark airport where she boards TWA jetliner, which is never seen again.

9:50 PM, EST: Entire S.A.C. fleet of 1200 jet bombers takes off for rendezvous over Newfoundland, where 72% are compelled to ditch as tankers fail to keep refueling rendezvous. (Orders committing the aircraft originate with S.A.C. commander, found to be a suicide.)

10:14 PM, EST: Submarine fusion explosion destroys 40% of New York City. Analysis of fallout indicates U.S. Navy Polaris missiles were detonated underwater in bay; by elimination it is deduced that the submarine was the *Ethan Allen.*

10:50 PM, EST: President's party assassinated by Secretary of Health, Education and Welfare; Secretary then dies on bayonet of Marine guard who furnished the grenade.

10:55 PM, EST Satellite stations observe great nuclear explosions in China and Tibet.

11:03 PM, EST: Heavily loaded munitions barges exploded near North Sea dikes of Holland; dikes breached, 1800 square miles of reclaimed land flooded out...

And so on. The incidents were countless. But before long, before even the C. I. A. had finished the first play through of the tapes, before their successors in the task identified *Disht dvornyet ilgt* as a Ukrainian dialect rendering of, My God, it works!—before all this, one fact was already apparent. There were many incidents scattered around the world, but not one of them took place in Russia itself.

WARSAW was ablaze, China pockmarked with blasts, East Berlin demolished along with its western sector, in eight rounds fired from a U.S. Army nuclear cannon. But the U.S.S.R. had not suffered at all, as far as could be told by the prying eyes in orbit; and that fact was reason enough for it to suffer very greatly very soon.

Within minutes of this discovery what remained of the military strength of the Western world was roaring through airless space toward the most likely targets of the East.

One unscathed missile base in Alaska completed a full shoot, seven missiles with fusion warheads. The three American bases that survived at all in the Mediterranean fired what they had. Even Britain, which had already watched the fire-tails of the American missiles departing on suicide missions, managed to resurrect its own two prototype Blue Streaks from their racks, where they had moldered since the cancellation of the British missile program. One of these museum-pieces destroyed itself in launching, but the other chugged painfully across the sky, the tortoise following the flight of the hares. It arrived a full half-hour after the newer, hotter missiles. It might as well not have bothered. There was not much left to destroy.

It was fortunate for the Communists that most of the Western arsenal had already spent itself in suicide. What was left wiped out Moscow, Leningrad and nine other cities. It was even fortunate for the whole world, for this was the Apocalypse they had dreaded, every possible nuclear weapon committed. But the circumstances were such—hasty orders, often at once recalled; confusion; panic—that most were unfused, many others merely tore great craters in the quickly healing surface of the sea. The fallout was locally murderous but quite spotty.

And the conventional forces invading Russia found nothing to fight. The Russians were as confused as they were. There were not many survivors of the very top brass, and no one seemed to know just what had happened.

Was the Secretary of the C.P., U.S.S.R. behind that terrible brief agony? As he was dead before it was over, there was no way to tell. More than a quarter of a billion lives went into mushroom-shaped clouds, and nearly half of them were Russian, Latvian, Tatar and Kalmuck. The Peace Commission squabbled for a month, until the breakdown of communications cut them off from their governments and each other; and in that way, for a time, there was peace.

THIS was the sort of peace that was left, thought Chandler looking around at the queer faces and queerer surroundings, the peace of medieval baronies, cut off from the world, untouched where the rain of fallout had passed by but hardly civilized any more. Even his own hometown, trying to take his life in a form of law, reduced at last to torture and exile to cast him out, was not the civilization he had grown up in but something new and ugly.

There was a great deal of talk he did not understand because he could not quite hear it, though they looked at him. Then Guy, with the gun, led him up to the front of the room. They had constructed an improvised platform out of plywood panels resting on squat, heavy boxes that looked like empty ammunition crates. On the dais was a dentist's chair, bolted to the plywood; and in the chair, strapped in, baby spotlights on steel-tube frames glaring on her, was a girl. She looked at Chandler with regretting eyes but did not speak.

"Stranger, get up there," said Guy, prodding him from behind, and Chandler took a wooden chair next to the girl.

"People of Orphalese," cried the teen-age cutie named Meggie, "we have two more brands to save from the imps!"

The men and women in the audience cackled or shrilled, "Save them! Save them!" They all had a look of invisible uniforms, Chandler saw, like baseball players in the lobby of a hotel or soldiers in a diner outside the gate of their post; they were all of a type. Their type was something strange. Some were tall, some short; there were old, fat, lean and young around them; but they all wore about them a look of glowing excitement, muted by an aura of suffering and pain. They wore, in a word, the look of bigots.

The bound girl was not one of them. She might have been twenty years old or as much as thirty. She might have been pretty. It was hard to tell—no makeup, her hair strung raggedly to her neck, and her face was drawn into a tight, lean line. It was her eyes that were alive. She saw Chandler and she was sorry for him. And he saw, as he turned to look at her, that she was manacled to the dentist's chair.

"People of Orphalese," chanted Guy, standing behind Chandler with the muzzle of the gun against his neck, "the *meeting* of the

Orphalese Self-Preservation *Society* will now come to *order.*" There was an approving, hungry murmur from the audience.

"Well, people of *Orphalese,*" Guy went on in his singsong, "the agenda for the *day* is first the salvation of we *Orphalese* on Mc-Guire's *Mountain.*"

("All saved, all of us saved," rolled a murmur from the congregation.") A lean, redheaded man bounded to the platform and fussed with the stand of spotlights, turning one of them full on Chandler.

"People of Orphalese, as we are *saved*, do I have your consent to *pass on* and proceed to the next order of *business?*"

("Consent, consent, consent," rolled the echo.)

"And then the *second* item of business is to *welcome* and bring to grace these two newly *found* and adopted *souls.*"

The congregation shouted variously: "Bring them to grace! Save them from the imps! Keep Orphalese from the taint of the beast!"

Evidently Guy was satisfied. He nodded and became more chatty. "Okay, people of Orphalese, let's get down to it. We got two new ones, like I say. Their spirits have gone wandering on the wind, or anyway one of them has, and you all know the etcetera. They have committed a wrong unto others and therefore unto themselves. Herself, I mean. Course, the other one could have a flame spirit in him too." He stared severely at Chandler. "Boys, keep an eye on him, why don't you?" he said to two men in the front row, surrendering his gun. "Meggie, you tell about the female one."

The teen-aged girl stepped forward and said, in a conversational tone but with modest pride, "People of Orph'lese, well, I was walking down the cut and I heard this car coming. Well, I was pretty surprised, you know. I had to figure what to do. You all know what the trouble is with cars."

"The imps!" cried a woman of forty with a face like a catfish.

The girl nodded. "Most prob'ly. Well, I—I mean, people of Orph'lese, well, I was by the switchback where we keep the chevvy-freeze hid, so I just waited till I saw it slowing down for the curve—me out of sight, you know—and I rolled the chevvy-freeze out nice and it caught the wheels. Right over!" she cried gleefully.

"Off the shoulder, people of Orph'lese, and into the ditch and over, and I didn't give it a chance to burn. I cut the switch and I had her! I put a knife into her back, just a little, about a quarter of an inch, maybe. Her pain was the breakin' of the shell that enclosed her understanding, like it says. I figured she was all right then because she yelled but I brought her along that way. Then Guy took care of her until we got the synod. Oh," she remembered, "and her tongue staggered a little without purpose while he was putting it on, didn't it, Guy?" The bearded man nodded, grinning, and lifted up the girl's foot. Incredulously, Chandler saw that it was bound tight with a three-foot length of barbed wire, wound and twisted like a tourniquet, the blood black and congealed around it. He lifted his shocked eyes to meet the girl's. She only looked at him, with pity and understanding.

Guy patted the foot and let it go. "I didn't have any more C-clamps, people of Orphalese," he apologized, "but it looks all right at that. Well, let's see. We got to make up our minds about these two, I guess—no, wait!" He held up his hand as a murmur began. "First thing is, we ought to read a verse or two."

He opened a purple-bound volume at random, stared at a page for a moment, moving his lips, and then read:

"Some of you say, 'It is the north wind who has woven the clothes we wear.'

"And I say, Aye, it was the north wind, but shame was his loom, and the softening of the sinews was his thread.

"And when his work was done he laughed in the forest."

Gently he closed the book, looking thoughtfully at the wall at the back of the room. He scratched his head. "Well, people of Orphalese," he said slowly, "they're laughing in the forest all right, I guarantee, but we've got one here that may be honest in the flesh, probably is, though she was a thief in the spirit. Right? Well, do we take her in or reject her, O people of Orphalese?"

The audience muttered to itself and then began to call out:

"Accept! Oh, bring in the brand! Accept and drive out the imp!"

"Fine," said the teen-ager, rubbing her hands and looking at the bearded man. "Guy, let her go." He began to release her from the chair. "You, girl stranger, what's your name?"

The girl said faintly, "Ellen Braisted."

"*Meggie,* my name is Ellen Braisted," corrected the teenager. "Always say the name of the person you're talkin' to in Orph'lese, that way we know it's you talkin', not a flame spirit or wanderer. Okay, go sit down." Ellen limped wordlessly down into the audience. "Oh, and people of Orph'lese," said Meggie, "the car's still there if we need it for anything. It didn't burn. Guy, you go on with this other fellow."

Guy stroked his beard and assessed Chandler, looking him over carefully. "Okay," he said. "People of Orphalese, the *third* order of business is to *welcome* or reject this *other* brand saved from the imps, as may be your *pleasure.*"

Chandler sat up straighter now that all of them were looking at him again; but it wasn't quite his turn, at that, because there was an interruption. Guy never finished. From the valley, far below, there was a sudden mighty thunder, rolling among the mountains. The windows blew in with a crystalline crash.

THE room erupted into confusion, the audience leaping from their seats, running to the broad windows, Guy and the teenage girl seizing rifles, everyone in motion at once.

Chandler straightened, then sat down again. The redheaded man guarding him was looking away. It would be quite possible to grab his gun, run, get away from these maniacs. Yet he had nowhere to go. They might be crazy, but they seemed to have organization.

They seemed, in fact, to have worked out, on whatever crazed foundation of philosophy, some practical methods for coping with possession. He decided to stay, wait and see.

And at once he found himself leaping for the gun.

No. Chandler didn't find himself attacking the redheaded man. He found his *body* doing it; Chandler had nothing to do with it. It was the helpless compulsion he had felt before, that had nearly cost him his life; his body active and urgent and his mind completely cut off from it. He felt his own muscles move in ways he had not planned, observed himself leap forward, felt his own fist strike at the back of the redheaded man's ear. The man went spinning, the gun went flying, Chandler's body leaped after it, with Chandler a prisoner in his own brain, watching, horrified and helpless. And he had the gun!

He caught it in the hand that was his own hand, though someone else was moving it; he raised it and half-turned. He was suddenly conscious of a fusillade of gunfire from the roof, and a scattered echo of guns all round the outside of the house. Part of him was surprised, another alien part was not. He started to shoot the teen-aged girl in the back of the head, silently shouting *No!*

His fingers never pulled the trigger.

He caught a second's glimpse of someone just beside him, whirled and saw the girl, Ellen Braisted, limping swiftly toward him with her barbed-wire amulet loose and catching at her feet. In her hands was an axe-handle club caught up from somewhere. She struck at Chandler's head, with a face like an eagle's, impersonal and determined. The blow caught him and dazed him, and from behind someone else struck him with something else. He went down.

He heard shouts and firing, but he was stunned. He felt himself dragged and dropped. He saw a cloudy, misty girl's face hanging over him; it receded and returned. Then a frightful blistering pain in his hand startled him back into full consciousness.

It was the girl, Ellen, still there, leaning over him and, oddly, weeping. And the pain in his hand was the burning flame of a kitchen match. Ellen was doing it, his wrist in one hand, a burning match held to it with the other.

CHAPTER FOUR

CHANDLER yelled hoarsely, jerking his hand away.

She dropped the match and jumped up, stepping on the flame and watching him. She had a butcher knife that had been caught between her elbow and her body while she burned him. Now she put her hand on the knife, waiting. "Does it hurt?" she demanded tautly.

Chandler howled, with incredulity and rage: "Damn it, yes! What did you expect?"

"I expected it to hurt," she agreed. She watched him for a moment more and then, for the first time since he had seen her, she smiled. It was a small smile, but a beginning. A fusillade of shots from outside wiped it away at once. "Sorry," she said. "I had to do that. Please trust me."

"*Why* did you have to burn my hand?"

"House rules," she said. "Keeps the flame-spirits out, you know. They can't stand pain." She took her hand off the knife warily. "It still hurts, doesn't it?"

"It still does, yes," nodded Chandler bitterly, and she lost interest in him and got up, looking about the room. Three of the Orphalese were dead, or seemed to be from the casual poses in which they lay draped across a chair on the floor. Some of the others might have been freshly wounded, though it was hard to tell the casualties from the others in view of the Orphalese custom of self-inflicted pain. There was still firing going on outside and overhead, and a shooting-gallery smell of burnt powder in the air. The girl, Ellen Braisted, limped back with the butcher knife held carelessly in one hand. She was followed by the teen-ager, who wore a smile of triumph—and, Chandler noticed for the first time, a sort of tourniquet of barbed wire on her left forearm, the flesh puffy red around it. "Whopped 'em," she said with glee, and pointed a .22 rifle at Chandler.

Ellen Braisted said, "Oh, he—*Meggie,* I mean, he's all right." She pointed at his burned palm. Meg approached him with competent care, the rifle resting on her good right forearm and aimed at him as she examined his burn. She pursed her lips and looked at his face. "All right, Ellen, I guess he's clean. But you want to burn 'em deeper'n that. Never pays to go easy, just means we'll have to do something else to 'im tomorrow."

"The hell you will," thought Chandler, and all but said it; but reason stopped him. In Rome he would have to do Roman deeds. Besides, maybe their ideas worked. Besides, he had until tomorrow to make up his mind about what he wanted to do.

"Ellen, show him around," ordered the teen-ager. "I got no time myself. Shoosh! Almost got us that time, Ellen. Got to be more careful, cause the white-handed aren't clean, you know." She strutted away, the rifle at trail. She seemed to be enjoying herself very much.

THE name of the girl in the barbed-wire bracelet was Ellen Braisted. She came from Lehigh County, Pennsylvania, and Chandler's first wonder was what she was doing nearly three thousand miles from home.

Nobody liked to travel much these days. One place was as bad as another, except that in the place where you were known you could perhaps count on friends and as a stranger you were probable fair game anywhere else. Of course, there was one likely reason for travel.

She didn't like to talk about it, that was clear, but that was the reason. She had been possessed. When the teen-ager trapped her car the day before she had been the tool of another's will. She had had a dozen submachine guns in the trunk and she had meant to deliver them to a party of hunters in a valley just south of McGuire's Mountain. Chandler said, with some effort, "I must have been—"

"*Ellen*, I must have been," she corrected.

"Ellen, I must have been possessed too, just now. When I grabbed the gun."

"Of course. First time?"

He shook his head. For some reason the brand on his forehead began to throb.

"Well, then you know. Look out here, now."

They were at the great pier windows that looked out over the valley. Down below was the river, an arc of the railroad tracks, the wooded mountainside he had scaled. "Over there, Chandler." She was pointing to the railroad bridge.

Wispy gray smoke drifted off southward toward the stream. The freight train Chandler had ridden on had been stopped, all that time, in the middle of the bridge. The explosion that blew out their windows had occurred when another train plowed into it— evidently at high speed. It seemed that one of the trains had carried some sort of chemicals. The bridge was a twisted mess.

"A diversion, Chandler," said Ellen Braisted. "They wanted us looking that way. Then they attacked from up the mountain."

"Who?"

Ellen looked surprised. "The men that crashed the trains...if they *are* men. The ones who possessed me—and you—and the hunters. They don't like these Orphalese, I think. Maybe they're a little afraid of them. I think the Orphalese have a pretty good idea of how to fight them."

Chandler felt a sudden flash of sensation along his nerves. For a moment he thought he had been possessed again, and then he knew it for what it was. It was hope. "Ellen, I never thought of fighting them. I thought that was given up two years ago."

"So maybe you agree with me? Maybe you think it's worth while sticking with the Orphalese?"

Chandler allowed himself the contemplation of what hope meant. To find someone in this world who had a *plan!* Whatever the plan was. Even if it was a bad plan. He didn't think specifically of himself, or the brand on his forehead or the memory of the body of his wife. What he thought of was the prospect of thwarting—not even defeating, merely hampering or annoying was enough!—the imps, the "flame creatures," the pythons, devils, incubi or demons who had destroyed a world he had thought very fair.

"If they'll have me," he said, "I'll stick with them, all right. Where do I go to join?"

IT was not hard to join at all.

Meg chattily informed him that he was already practically a member. "Chandler, we got to watch everybody strange, you know. See why, don't you? Might have a flame spirit in 'em, no fault of theirs, but look how they could mess us up. But now we know you don't, so— What do you mean, how do we know? Cause you *did* have one when you busted loose in there. Can't have two at a time, you know. Think we couldn't tell the difference?"

The interrupted meeting was resumed after the place had been tidied up and the dead buried. There had been four of the hunters, and even without their submachine guns they had succeeded in killing eight Orphalese. But it was not all loss to the Orphalese, because two of the hunters were still alive, though wounded, and under the rules of this chessboard the captured enemy became a friend.

Guy had suffered a broken jaw in the scuffle and another man presided, a fat youth who favored a bandaged leg. He limped to his feet, grimacing and patting his leg. "O Orphalese and brothers," he said, "we have lost friends, but we have won a test. Praise the Prophet, we will be spared to win again, and to drive the imps of fire out of our world. Meggie, you going to tie these folks up?" The girl proudly ordered one of the hunters into the spotlighted dentist's chair, another into a wing chair that was hastily moved onto the platform. The men were bleeding and hurt, but they had clearly been abandoned by their possessors. They watched with puzzlement and fear.

"Walter, they're okay now," Meg reported as others finished tying up the hunters. "Oh, wait a minute." She advanced on Chandler. "Chandler, I'm sorry. You sit down there, hear?"

Chandler suffered himself to be bound to a camp chair on the platform and Walter took a drink of wine and opened the ornate book that was before him on the rostrum.

"Meg, thanks. Guy, I hope I do this as good as you do. Let me read you a little. Let's see." He put on his steel-rimmed glasses and read:

"Much in you is still man, and much in you is not yet man, but a shapeless pigmy that walks asleep in the mist searching for its own awakening."

He closed the book, looked with satisfaction at Guy and said: "Do you understand that, new friends? They are the words of the Prophet, who men call Kahlil Gibran. For the benefit of the new folks I ought to say that he died this fleshly life quite a good number of years ago, but his vision was unclouded. Like we say, we are the sinews that batter the flame spirits but he is our soul." There was an antiphonal murmur from the audience and Walter flipped the pages again rapidly, obviously looking for a familiar passage. "People of Orphalese, here we are now. This's what he says. 'What is this that has torn our world apart?' The Prophet says: "It is life in quest of life, in bodies that fear the grave." Now, honestly, nothing could be clearer than that, people of Orphalese and friends! We got something taking possession of us, see? What is it? Well, he says here, people of Orphalese and friends, 'It is a flame spirit in you ever gathering more of itself.' Now, what the heck! Nobody can blame *us* for what a flame spirit *in* us does! So the first thing we got to learn, friends—and people of Orphalese—is, we aren't to blame. And the second thing is, we *are* to blame!"

He turned and grinned at Chandler kindly, while the chorus of responses came from the room, "Like here," he said, "people of Orphalese, the Prophet says *everybody* is guilty. 'The murdered is not unaccountable for his own murder, and the robbed is not blameless in being robbed. The righteous is not innocent of the deeds of the wicked, and the white-handed is not clean in the doings of the felon.' You see what he's getting at? We all got to take the responsibility for *everything*—and that means we got to suffer—but we don't have to worry about any special things we did when some flame spirit or wanderer, like, took us over.

"But we do have to suffer, people of Orphalese." His expression became grim. "Our beloved founder, Guy, who's sitting there doing a little extra suffering now, was favored enough to understand these things in the very beginning, when he himself was seized by these imps. And it is all in this book! Like it says, 'Your pain is self-chosen. It is the bitter potion by which the physician within you heals your sick self.' Ponder on that, people of Orphalese—and friends. No, I mean really ponder," he explained, glancing at the bound "friends" on the platform. "We always do that for a minute. Ada there will play us some music so we can ponder."

CHANDLER shifted uncomfortably, while an old woman crippled by arthritis began fumbling a tune out of an electric organ. The burn Ellen Braisted had given him was beginning to hurt badly. If only these people were not such obvious *nuts*, he thought, he would feel a lot better about casting his lot in with them. But maybe it took lunatics to do the job. Sane people hadn't accomplished much.

And anyway he had very little choice…

"Ada, that's enough," ordered the fat youth. "Meg, come on up here. People of Orphalese, now you can listen again while Meg explains to the new folks how all this got started, seeing Guy's in no condition to do it."

The teen-ager marched up to the platform and took the parade rest position learned in some high-school debating society—in the days when there were debating societies and high schools. "Ladies and gentlemen, well, let's start at the beginning. Guy tells this better'n I do, of course, but I guess I remember it all pretty well too. I ought to. I was in on it and all." She grimaced and said, "Well, anyway, ladies and gentlemen—people of Orph'lese—the way Guy organized this Orphalese self-protection society was, like Walter says, he was possessed. The only difference between Guy and you and me was that he knew what to do about it, because he read the book, you see. Not that that helped him at first, when he was took over. He was really seized. Yes, people of Orph'lese, he was taken and while his whole soul and brain and body was under the influence of some foul wanderer fiend from hell he did things that, ladies and gentlemen of Orph'lese, I wouldn't want to tell you. He was a harp in the hand of the mighty, as it says. Couldn't help it, not however much he tried. Only while he was doing—the things—he happened to catch his hand in a gas flame and, well, you can see it was pretty bad." With a deprecatory smile Guy held up a twisted hand. "And, do you know, he was free of his imp right then and there! Now, Guy is a scientist, people of Orph'lese, he worked for the telephone company, and he not only had that training in the company school but he had read the book, you see, and he put two and two together. Oh, and he's my uncle, of course. I'm proud of him. I've always loved him, and even when he—when he was not one with himself, you know, when he was doing those terrible things to me, I knew it wasn't Uncle Guy that was doing them, but something else. I didn't know what, though. And when he told me he had figured out the Basic Rule, I went along with him every bit. I knew Guy wasn't wrong, and what he said was from Scripture. Imps fear pain! So we got to love it. That one I know by heart, all right: 'Could you keep your heart from wonder at the daily miracles of your life, your pain would not seem less wondrous than your joy.' That's what it says, right? So that's why we got to hurt ourselves, people of Orph'lese—and new brothers—because the wanderers don't like it when we hurt and they leave us alone. Simple's that.

"Well—" the girl's face stiffened momentarily—"I knew *I* wasn't going to be seized. So Guy and I got Else, that's the other girl he'd been doing things to, and we knew she wasn't going to be taken either. Not if the imps feared pain like Guy said, because," she said solemnly, "I want to tell you Guy hurt us pretty bad.

"And then we came out here, and found this place, and ever since then we've been adding brothers and sisters. It's been slow, of course, because not many people come this way any more, and we've had to kill a lot. Yes, we have. Sometimes the possessed just can't be saved, but—"

Abruptly her face changed.

Suddenly alert, her face years older, she glanced around the room. Then she relaxed.

And screamed.

GUY leaped up. Hoarsely, his voice almost inarticulate as he tried to talk with his broken jaw, he cried, "Wha...Wha's...*matter*, Meg?"

"Uncle Guy!" she wailed. She plunged off the platform and flung herself into his arms, crying hysterically.

"Wha?"

She sobbed, "I could feel it! They *took* me. Guy, you promised me they couldn't!"

He shook his head, dazed, staring at her as though she were indeed possessed—still possessed, and telling him some fearful great lie to destroy his hopes. He seemed unable to comprehend what she had said. One of the hunters bellowed in stark fear: "For God's sake, untie us! Give us a chance, anyway!" Chandler yelled agreement. In one split second everyone in the room had been transmuted by terror into something less than human. No one seemed capable of any action. Slowly the plump youth who had presided moved over to the hunter bound in the dentist's chair and began to fumble blindly at the knots. Ellen Braisted dropped her head into her hands and began to shake.

The cruelty of the moment was that they had all tasted hope. Chandler writhed wildly against his ropes, his mind racing out of control. The world had become a hell for everyone, but a bearable hell until the promise of a chance to end it gave them a full sight of what their lives had been. Now that that was dashed they were far worse off than before.

Walter finished with the hunter and lethargically began to pick at Chandler's bonds. His face was slack and unseeing.

Then it, too, changed.

The plump youth stood up sharply, glanced about, and walked off the platform.

Ellen Braisted raised her face from her hands and, her eyes streaming, quietly stood up and followed. The old lady with the arthritis about-faced and limped with them. Chandler stared, puzzled, and then comprehended.

They were marching toward the corner of the room where the rifles were stacked. "Possessed!" Chandler bellowed, the words tasting of acid as they ripped out of his throat. "Stop them! You——Guy—look!" He flailed wildly at his loosened bonds, lunged, tottered and toppled, chair and all, crashingly off the platform.

The three possessed ones did not need to hurry. They had all the time in the world. They were already reaching out for the rifles when Chandler shouted. Economically they turned, raising the butts to their shoulders, and began to fire at the Orphalese. It was a queerly frightening sight to see the arthritic organist, with a face like a relaxed executioner, take quick aim at Guy and, with a thirty-thirty shell, blow his throat out. Three shots, and the nearest three of the congregation were dead. Three more, and others went down, while the remainder turned and tried to run. It was like a slaughter of vermin. They never had a chance.

When every Orphalese except themselves was down on the floor, dead, wounded or, like Chandler, overlooked, the arthritic lady took careful aim at Ellen Braisted and the plump youth and shot them neatly in the temples. They didn't try to prevent her. With expressions that seemed almost impatient they presented their profiles to her aim.

Then the arthritic lady glanced leisurely about, fired into the stomach of a wounded man who was trying to rise, reloaded her rifle for insurance and began to search the bodies of the nearest dead. She was looking for matches. When she found them, she tugged weakly at the upholstery on a couch, swore and began methodically to rip and crumple pages out of Kahlil Gibran. When she had a heap of loose papers piled against the dais she pitched the remainder of the book out of the window, knelt and ignited the crumpled heap.

She stood watching the fire, her expression angry and impatient, tapping her foot.

The crumpled pages burned briskly. Before they died the wooden dais was beginning to catch. Laboriously the old lady toted folding chairs to pile on the blaze until it was roaring handsomely.

She watched it for several minutes, until it was a great orange pillar of fire sweeping to the ceiling, until the drapes on the wall behind were burning and the platform was a holocaust, until the noise of crackling flame and the beginning of plaster falling from the high ceiling proved that there was no likelihood of the fire going out and, indeed, no way to put it out without a complete fire department arriving on the scene at once.

The old lady's expression cleared. She nodded to herself. She then put the muzzle of the rifle in her mouth and, with her thumb, pulled the trigger that blew the top of her head off. The body fell into the flames, but it was by then already dead.

CHANDLER had not been shot, but he was very near to roasting. Walter had released one hand and, while the possessed woman's attention was elsewhere, Chandler had worked on the other knots.

When he saw her commit suicide he redoubled his efforts. It was incredible to him that his life had been saved, and he knew that if he escaped the flames he still had nothing to live for—that blasted brief hope had broken his spirit—but his fingers had a will of their own.

He lay there, struggling, while great black clouds of smoke, orange painted from the flames, gathered under the high ceiling, while the thunder of falling lumps of plaster sounded like a child heaving volumes of the Encyclopedia Britannica down a flight of stairs, while the heat and shortage of oxygen made him breathe in violent spasms. Then he cried out sharply and stumbled to his feet. It was only a matter of moments before he was out of the house, but it was very nearly not time enough.

Behind him was a great, sustained crash. He thought it must have been the furniture on the upper floor toppling through the burned-out ceiling of the hall. He turned and looked.

It was dark, and now every window on the side of the house facing him was lighted. It was as though some mad householder had decided to equip his rooms only with orange lights, orange lights that flickered and moved. For a second Chandler thought there were still living people in the rooms—shapes moved and cavorted at the windows, as though they were gathering up possessions or waving wildly for help. But it was only the drapes, aflame, tossed about in the fierce heat.

Chandler sighed and turned away.

Pain was not a sure defense after all. Evidently it was only an annoyance to the possessors...whoever, or whatever, they might be. As soon as they had become suspicious they had exerted themselves and destroyed the Orphalese. He listened and looked about, but no one else moved. He had not expected anyone. He had been sure that he was the only survivor.

He began to walk down the hill toward the wrecked railway bridge, turning only when a roar told him that the roof of the house had fallen in. A tulip of flame a hundred feet tall rose above the standing walls, and above that a shower of floating red-orange sparks, heat-borne, drifting up and away and beginning to settle all over the mountainside. Many were still red when they landed, a few still flaming. It was a distinct risk that the trees would begin to burn, and then he would be in fresh danger. So great was his stupor that he did not even hurry.

By a plowed field he flung himself to the ground.

He could go no farther because he had nowhere to go. He had had two homes and he had been driven from both of them. He had had hope twice, and twice he had been damned.

He lay on his back, with the burning house mumbling and crackling in the distance, and stared up at the orange-lit tops of the trees and, past them, the stars. Over his left shoulder Deneb chased Vega across the sky; toward his feet something moved between the bright rosy dot that was Antares and another, the same brightness and hue—Mars? He spent several moments wondering if Mars were in that part of the heavens. Then he looked again for the tiny moving point that had crossed the claws of the Scorpion, but it was gone. A satellite, maybe. Although there were few of them left that the naked eye could hope to see. And there would never be any more, because the sort of accumulated wealth of nations that threw rockets into the sky was forever spent.

It was probably an airplane, he thought drowsily, and drifted off to sleep without realizing how remote even that possibility had become... He woke up to find that he was getting to his feet.

Once again an interloper tenanted his brain. He tried to interfere, for he could not help it, although he knew how useless it was, but his own neck muscles turned his head from side to side, his own eyes looked this way and that, his own hand reached down for a dead branch that lay on the ground, then hesitated and withdrew. His body stood motionless for a second, the lips moving, the larynx mumbling to itself. He could almost hear words. Chandler felt like a fly in amber, a prisoner in his own brainbox. He was not surprised when his legs moved to carry him back toward the destroyed building, now a fakir's bed of white-hot coals with brush fires spattered around it. He thought he knew why. It seemed very likely that what possessor had him was a sort of cleanup squad, tidying up the loose ends of the slaughter; he expected that his body's errand was to destroy itself, and thus him, as all the Orphalese had been destroyed.

CHAPTER FIVE

CHANDLER'S body carried him rapidly toward the house. Now and then it paused and glanced about. It seemed to be weighing some shortcut in its errand; but always it resumed its climb.

Chandler could sympathize with it, in a way. He still felt every pain from burn, brand and wound; as they neared the embers of the building the heat it threw off intensified them all. He could not be a comfortable body to inhabit for long. He was almost sympathetic because his tenant could not find a convenient weapon with which to fulfill his purpose.

When it seemed they could get no closer without the skin of his face crackling and bursting into flame his body halted.

Chandler could feel his muscles gathering for what would be the final leap into the auto-da-fe. His feet took a short step—and slipped. His body stumbled and recovered itself; his mouth swore thickly in a language he did not know.

Then his body hesitated, glanced at the ground, paused again and bent down. It had tripped on a book. It picked the book up, and Chandler saw that it was the Orphalese copy of Gibran's *The Prophet*.

Chandler's body stood poised for a moment, in an attitude of thought. Then it sat down, in the play of heat from the coals. It was a moment before Chandler realized he was free. He tested his legs; they worked; he got up, turned and began to walk away.

He had traveled no more than a few yards when he stumbled slightly, as though shifting gears, and felt the tenant in his mind again.

He continued to walk away from the building, down toward the road. Once his arm raised the book he still carried and his eyes glanced down, as if for reassurance that it was the same book. That was the only clue he was given as to what had happened and it was not much. It was as though his occupying power, whatever it was, had gone—somewhere—to think things over, perhaps to ask a question of an unimaginable companion, and then returned with an altered purpose. As time passed, Chandler began to receive additional clues, but he was in little shape to fit them together, for his body was near exhaustion.

He walked to the road, and waited, rigid, until a panel truck came bouncing along. He hailed it, his arms making a sign he did not understand, and when it stopped he addressed the driver in a language he did not speak. *"Shto,"* said the driver, a somber-faced Mexican in dungarees. *"Ja nie jestem Ruska. Czego pragniesh?"*

"Czy ty jedziesz to Los Angeles?" asked Chandler's mouth.

"Nyet. Acapulco."

Chandler's voice argued, *"Wes na* Los Angeles."

"Nyet." The voices droned on. Chandler lost interest in the argument and was only relieved when it seemed somehow to be settled and he was herded into the back of the truck. The somber Mexican locked him in; he felt the truck begin to move; his tenant left him, and he was at once asleep.

He woke long enough to find himself standing in the mist of early dawn at a crossroads. In a few minutes another car came by, and his voice talked earnestly with the driver for a moment. Chandler got in, was released, slept again and woke to find himself free and abandoned, sprawled across the back seat of the car, which was parked in front of a building marked Los Angeles International Airport.

CHANDLER got out of the car and strolled around, stretching. He realized he was very hungry.

No one was in sight. The field showed clear signs of having been through the same sort of destruction that had visited every major communications facility in the world. Part of the building before him was smashed flat and showed signs of having been burned. He saw projecting aluminum members, twisted and scorched but still visibly aircraft parts. Apparently a transport had crashed into the building. Burned-out cars littered the parking lot and what had once been a green lawn. They seemed to have been bulldozed out of the way, but not an inch farther than was necessary to clear the approach roads.

To his right, as he stared out onto the field, was a strange looking construction on three legs, several stories high. It did not seem to serve any useful purpose. Perhaps it had been a sort of luxury restaurant at one time, like the Space Needle from the old Seattle Fair, but now it too was burned out and glassless in its windows. The field itself was swept bare except for two or three parked planes in the bays, but he could see wrecked transports lining the approach strips. All in all, Los Angeles International Airport appeared to be serviceable, but only just.

He wondered where all the people were.

Distant truck noises answered part of the question. An Army six by six came bumping across a bridge that led from the takeoff strips to this parking area of the airport. Five men got out next to one of the ships. They glanced at him but did not speak as they began loading crates of some sort of goods from the truck into the aircraft, a four-engine, swept-wing jet of what looked to Chandler like an obsolete model. Perhaps it was one of the early Boeings. There hadn't been many of those in use at the time the troubles began, too big and fast for short hops, too slow to compete over long distances with the rockets. But, of course, with all the destruction, and with no new aircraft being built anywhere in the world any more, no doubt they were as good as could be found.

The truckmen did not seem to be possessed; they worked with the normal amount of grunting and swearing, pausing to wipe sweat away or to scratch an itch. They showed neither the intense malevolent concentration nor the wide-eyed idiot curiosity of those whose bodies were no longer their own. Chandler settled the woolen cap over the brand on his forehead, to avoid unpleasantness, and drifted over toward them.

They stopped work and regarded him. One of them said something to another, who nodded and walked toward Chandler. "What do you want?" he demanded warily.

"I don't know. I was going to ask you the same question, I guess."

The man scowled. "Didn't your exec tell you what to do?"

"My what?"

The man paused, scratched and shook his head. "Well, stay away from us. This is an important shipment, see? I guess you're all right or you couldn't've got past the guards, but I don't want you messing us up. Got enough trouble already. I don't know why," he said in the tones of an old grievance, "we can't get the execs to let us *know* when they're going to bring somebody in. It wouldn't hurt them! Now here we got to load and fuel this ship and, for all I know, you've got half a ton of junk around somewhere that you're going to load onto it. How do I know how much fuel it'll take? No weather, naturally. So if there's headwinds it'll take full tanks, but if there's extra cargo I—"

"The only cargo I brought with me that I can think of is a book," said Chandler. "Weighs maybe a pound. You think I'm supposed to get on that plane?"

The man grunted non-committally.

"All right, suit yourself. Listen, is there any place I can get something to eat?"

The man considered. "Well, I guess we can spare you a sandwich. But you wait here. I'll bring it to you."

He went back to the truck. A moment later one of the others brought Chandler two cold hamburgers wrapped in waxed paper, but would answer no questions.

CHANDLER ate every crumb, sought and found a washroom in the wrecked building, came out again and sat in the sun, watching the loading crew. He had become quite a fatalist. It did not seem that it was intended he should die immediately, so he might as well live.

There were large gaps in his understanding, but it seemed clear to Chandler that these men, though not possessed, were in some way working for the possessors. It was a distasteful concept; but on second thought it had reassuring elements. It was evidence that whatever the "execs" were, they were very possibly human beings—or, if not precisely human, at least shared the human trait of working by some sort of organized effort toward some sort of a goal. It was the first non-random phenomenon he had seen in connection with the possessors, barring the short term tactical matters of mass slaughter and destruction. It made him feel—what he tried at once to suppress, for he feared another destroying frustration—a touch of hope.

The men finished their work but did not leave. Nor did they approach Chandler, but sat in the shade of their truck, waiting for something. He drowsed and was awakened by a distant sputter of a single-engined Aerocoupe that hopped across the building behind him, turned sharply and came down with a brisk little run in the parking bay itself.

From one side the pilot climbed down and from the other two men lifted, with great care, a wooden crate, small but apparently heavy. They stowed it in the jet while the pilot stood watching; then the pilot and one of the other men got into the crew compartment. Chandler could not be sure, but he had the impression that the truckman who entered the plane was no longer his own master. His movements seemed more sure and confident, but above all it was the mute, angry eyes with which his fellows regarded him that gave Chandler grounds for suspicion. He had no time to worry about that; for in the same breath he felt himself occupied once more.

He did not rise. His own voice said to him, "You. Votever you name, you fellow vit de book! You go get de book verever you pud it and get on dat ship dere, you see?" His eyes turned toward the waiting aircraft. "And don't forget de book!"

He was released. "I won't," he said automatically, and then realized that there was no longer anyone there to hear his answer.

When he retrieved the Gibran volume from the car and approached the plane the loading crew said nothing. Evidently they knew what he was doing—either because they too had been given instructions, or because they were used to such things. He paused at the wheeled stairs. "Listen," he said, "can you at least tell me where I'm going?"

The four remaining men looked at him silently, with the same angry, worried expression he had seen on their faces before. They did not answer, but after a moment one of them raised his arm and pointed.

West. Out toward the Pacific. Out toward some ten million square miles of nearly empty sea.

LONG before they reached their destination Chandler had reasoned what it must be. He was correct: It was the islands of Hawaii.

Chandler knew that the pilot and his co-opted partner were up forward, in the crew compartment, but the door was locked and he never saw them again. Apart from them he was the only living person on the plane.

The plane was lightly loaded with cargo of unidentifiable sorts. In the rear section, where once tourist-class passengers had eaten their complimentary tray meals and planned their vacations, the seats had been removed and a thin scatter of crates and boxes were strapped to the floor. In the luxury of the forward section Chandler sat, stared at the water and drowsed. He seemed to be always sleepy. Perhaps it was the consequence of his exertions; more likely it was a psychological phenomenon. He was beyond worry. He had reached that point in emotional fatigue when the sudden rattle of cannon fire or the enemy's banzai charge can no longer flood the blood with adrenaline. The glands are dry. The emotions have been triggered too often. Battle fatigue takes men in many different ways, but in Chandler it was only apathy. He not only could not worry, he could not even rouse himself to feel hunger, although the pricking of habit made him get up and search the flight kitchen, unsuccessfully, for food.

He had no idea how much time had passed when the hiss of the jets changed key.

The horizon dipped below the wingtip and straightened again, and he beheld land. He never saw the airfield, only water, then beach, then water again, then a few buildings. Then there was a roar of jets, with their clamshells deflecting their thrust forward to brake their speed, and then the wheels were on the ground. As the plane stopped he felt himself once more possessed. It was no longer terrifying—though Chandler was sure he was doomed.

Without knowing where he was going or why he picked up the ripped book, opened the cabin exit and stepped down onto the rolling steps that had immediately been brought into place. He was conscious of a horde of men swarming around the plane, stripping it of its cargo, and wondered briefly at the rush; but he could not stop to watch them, his legs carried him swiftly across a paved strip to where a police car was cruising.

Chandler cringed inside, instinctively, but his body did not falter as it stepped into the path of the car and raised its hand.

The police car jammed on its brakes. The policeman at the wheel, Chandler thought inside himself, looked startled, but he also looked resigned. "To de South Gate, quickly," said Chandler's lips, and he felt his legs carry him around to the door on the other side.

There was another policeman on the seat next to the driver. He leaped like a hare to get the door open and get out before Chandler's body got there. He made it with nothing to spare. "Jack, you go on, I'll tell Headquarters," he said hurriedly. The driver nodded without speaking. His lips were white. He reached over Chandler to close the door and made a sharp U-turn.

As soon as the car was moving Chandler felt himself able to move his lips again.

"I—" he said. "I don't know—"

"Friend," said the policeman, "kindly keep your mouth shut. 'South Gate,' the exec said, and South Gate is where I'm going."

Chandler shrugged and looked out the window…just in time to see the jet that had brought him to the islands once more lumbering into life. It crept, wobbling its wingtips, over the ground, picked up speed, roared across taxi strips and over rough ground and at last piled up against an ungainly looking foreign airplane, a Russian jet by its markings, in a thunderous crash and ball of flame as its fuel exploded. No one got out.

It seemed that traffic to Hawaii was all one way.

CHAPTER SIX

THEY roared through downtown Honolulu with the siren blaring and cars scattering out of the way. At seventy miles an hour they raced down a road by the sea. Chandler caught a glimpse of a sign that said "Hilo," but where or what "Hilo" might be he had no idea. Soon there were fewer cars; then there were none but their own. The road was a suburban highway lined with housing developments, shopping centers, palm groves and the occasional center of a small municipality, scattering helter-skelter together. There was a road like this extending in every direction from every city in the United States, Chandler thought; but this one was some-what altered. Something had been there before them. About a mile outside Honolulu's outer fringe, life was cut off as with a knife. There were no people on foot, and the only cars were rusted wrecks lining the roads. The lawns were ragged stands of weeds in front of the ranch-type homes.

It was evidently not allowed to live here.

Chandler craned his neck. His curiosity was becoming almost unbearable. He opened his mouth, but...

"I said shut up," rumbled the cop without looking at him.

There was a note in the policeman's voice that impressed Chandler. He did not quite know what it was, but it made him obey. They drove for another fifteen minutes in silence, then drew up before a barricade across the road.

Chandler got out. The policeman slammed the door behind him, ripping rubber off his tires with the speed of his U-turn and acceleration back toward Honolulu. He did not look at Chandler.

Chandler stood staring off after him, in bright warm sunlight with a reek of hibiscus and rotting palms in his nostrils. It was very quiet except for a soft scratchy sound of footsteps on gravel. As Chandler turned to face the man coming toward him, he realized he had learned one fact from the policeman after all. The cop was scared clear through.

Chandler said, "Hello," to the man who was approaching.

He too wore a uniform, but not that of the Honolulu city police. It was like U. S. Army suntans, but without insignia. Behind him were half a dozen others in the same dress, smoking, chatting, leaning against whatever was handy. The barricades themselves were impressively thorough. Barbed wire ran down the beach and out into the ocean; on the other side of the road, barbed wire ran clear out of sight along the middle of a side road. The gate itself was bracketed with machine-gun emplacements.

The guard waited until he was close to Chandler before speaking. "What do you want?" he asked without greeting. Chandler shrugged. "All right, just wait here," said the guard, and began to walk away again.

"Wait a minute! What am I waiting for?" The guard shook his head without stopping or turning. He did not seem very interested, and he certainly was not helpful.

Chandler put down the copy of *The Prophet* , which he had carried so far and sat on the ground, but again he had no long time to wait. One of the guards came toward him, with the purposeful movements Chandler had learned to recognize. Without speaking the guard dug into a pocket. Chandler jumped up instinctively, but it was only a set of car keys.

As Chandler took them the look in the guard's eyes showed the quick release of tension that meant he was free again; and in that same moment Chandler's own body was occupied once more.

He reached down and picked up the book. Quickly, but a little clumsily, his fingers selected a key, and his legs carried him toward a little French car parked just the other side of the barrier.

CHANDLER was learning at last the skills of allowing his body to have its own way. He couldn't help it in any event, so he was consciously disciplining himself to withdraw his attention from his muscles and senses. It involved queerly vertiginous problems. A hundred times a minute there was some unexpected body sway or movement of the hand, and his lagging, imprisoned mind would wrench at its unresponsive nerves to put out the elbow that would brace him, or to catch itself with a step. He had learned to ignore these things. The mind that inhabited his body had ways not his own of maintaining balance and reaching an objective, but they were equally sure.

He watched his own hands shifting the gears of the car. It was a make he had never driven, with a clutchless drive he did not understand, but the mind in his brain evidently understood it well enough. They picked up speed in great, gasoline-wasting surges.

Chandler began to form a picture of that mind. It belonged to an older man, from the hesitancy of its walk, and a testy one, from the heedless crash of the gears as it shifted. It drove with careless slapdash speed. Chandler's mind yelled and flinched in his brain as they rounded blind curves, where any casual other motorist would have been a catastrophe; but the hand on the wheel and the foot on the accelerator did not hesitate.

Beyond the South Gate the island of Oahu became abruptly wild.

There were beautiful homes, but there were also great, gap-toothed spaces where homes had once been and were no longer. It seemed that some monstrous Zoning Commissar had stalked through the island with an eraser, rubbing out the small homes, the cheap ones, the old ones; rubbing out the stores, rubbing out the factories. This whole section of the island had been turned into an exclusive residential park.

It was not uninhabited. Chandler thought he glimpsed a few people, though since the direction of his eyes was not his to control it was hard to be sure. And then the Renault turned into a lane, paved but narrow. Hardwood trees with some sort of blossoms, Chandler could not tell what, overhung it on both sides.

It meandered for a mile or so, turned and opened into a great vacant parking lot. The Renault stopped with a squeal of brakes in front of a door that was flanked by bronze plaques: *TWA Flight Message Center.*

Chandler caught sight of a skeletal towering form overhead, like a radio transmitter antenna, as his body marched him inside, up a motionless escalator, along a hall and into a room.

His muscles relaxed.

He glanced around and, from a huge couch beside a desk, a huge soft body stirred and, gasping, sat up. It was a very fat old man, almost bald, wearing a coronet of silvery spikes.

He looked at Chandler without much interest. "Vot's your name?" he wheezed. He had a heavy, ineradicable accent, like a Hapsburg or a Russian diplomat. Chandler recognized it readily. He had heard it often enough, from his own lips.

THE man's name was Koitska, he said in his accented wheeze. If he had another name he did not waste it on Chandler. He took as few words as possible to order Chandler to be seated and to be still.

Koitska squinted at the copy of Gibran's *The Prophet*. He did not glance at Chandler, but Chandler felt himself propelled out of his seat, to hand the book to Koitska, then returning. Koitska turned its remaining pages with an expression of bored repugnance, like a man picking off his arm. He seemed to be waiting for something.

A door closed on the floor below, and in a moment a girl came into the room.

She was tall, dark and not quite young. Chandler, struck by her beauty, was sure that he had seen her, somewhere, but could not place her face. She wore a coronet like the fat man's, intertwined in a complicated hairdo, and she got right down to business. "Chandler, is it? All right, love, what we want to know is what this is all about." She indicated the book.

A relief that was like pain crossed Chandler's mind. So that was why he was here! Whoever these people were, however they managed to rule men's minds, they were not quite certain of their perfect power. To them the sad, futile Orphalese represented a sort of annoyance—not important enough to be a threat—but something, which had proved inconvenient at one time, and therefore needed investigating. As Chandler was the only survivor they had deemed it worth their godlike whiles to transport him four thousand miles so that he might satisfy their curiosity.

Chandler did not hesitate in telling them all about the people of Orphalese. There was nothing worth concealing, he was quite sure. No debts are owed to the dead; and the Orphalese had proved on their own heads, at the last, that their ritual of pain was only an annoyance to the possessors, not a tactic that could long be used against them.

It took hardly five minutes to say everything that needed saying about Guy, Meggie and the other doomed and suffering inhabitants of the old house on the mountain.

Koitska hardly spoke. The girl was his interrogator, and sometimes translator as well, when his English was not sufficient to comprehend a point. With patient detachment she kept the story moving until Koitska with a bored shrug indicated he was through.

Then she smiled at Chandler and said, "Thanks, love. Haven't I seen you somewhere before?"

"I don't know. I thought the same thing about you."

"Oh, everybody's seen me. Lots of me. But—well, no matter. Good luck, love. Be nice to Koitska and perhaps he'll do as much for you." And she was gone.

Koitska lay unmoving on his couch for a few moments, rubbing a fat nose with a plump finger. "Hah," he said at last. Then, abruptly, "And now, de qvestion is, vot to do vit you, eh? I do not t'ink you can cook, eh?"

WITH unexpected clarity Chandler realized he was on trial for his life. "Cook? No, I'm afraid not. I mean, I can boil eggs," he said. "Nothing fancy."

"Hah," grumbled Koitska. "Vel. Ve need a couple, three doctors, but I do not t'ink you vould do."

Chandler shook his head. "I'm an electrical engineer," he said. "Or was."

"Vas?"

"I haven't had much practice. There has not been a great deal of call for engineers, the last year or two."

"Hah." Koitska seemed to consider.

"Vel," he said, "it could be…yes, it could be dat ve have a job for you. You go back downstairs and—no, vait." The fat man closed his eyes and Chandler felt himself seized and propelled down the stairs to what had once been a bay of a built-in garage. Now it was fitted up with workbenches and the gear of a radio ham's dreams.

Chandler walked woodenly to one of the benches. His own voice spoke to him. "Ve got here someplace—*da*, here is cirguit diagrams and de specs for a sqvare-vave generator. You know vot dat is? Write down de answer." Chandler, released with a pencil in his hand and a pad before him, wrote *Yes.* "Okay. Den you build vun for me. I areddy got vun but I vant another. You do dis in de city, not here. Go to Tripler, dey tells you dere vere you can work, vere to get parts, all dat. Couple days you come out here again, I see if I like how you build."

Clutching the thick sheaf of diagrams, Chandler felt himself propelled outside and back into the little car. The interview was over.

He wondered if he would be able to find his way back to Honolulu, but that problem was then postponed as he discovered he could not start the car. His own hands had already done so, of course, but it had been so quick and sure that he had not paid attention; now he found that the ignition key was marked only in French, which he could not speak. After trial and error he discovered the combination that would start the engine and unlock the steering wheel, and then gingerly he toured the perimeter of the lot until he found an exit road.

It was close to midnight, he judged. Stars were shining overhead; there was a rising moon. He then remembered, somewhat tardily, that he should not be seeing stars. The lane he had come in on had been overhung on both sides with trees.

A few minutes later he realized he was quite lost.

Chandler stopped the car, swore feelingly, got out and looked around.

There was nothing much to see. The roads bore no markers that made sense to him. He shrugged and rummaged through the glove compartment on the chance of a map; there was none, but he did find what he had almost forgotten, a half-empty pack of cigarettes. It had been—he counted—nearly a week since he had smoked. He lit up.

IT was a pleasant evening, too. He felt almost relaxed. He stood there, wondering just what might be about to happen next— with curiosity more than fear—and then he felt a light touch at his mind.

It was nothing, really. Or nothing that he could quite identify. It was though he had been nudged. It seemed that someone was about to usurp his body again, but that did not develop.

As he had about decided to forget it and get back in the car he saw headlights approaching.

A low, lean sports car slowed as it came near, stopping beside him, and a girl leaned out, almost invisible in the darkness. "There you are love," she said cheerfully. "Thought I spotted someone. Lost?"

She had a coronet, and Chandler recognized her. It was the girl who had interrogated him. "I guess I am," he admitted.

The girl leaned forward. "Come in, dear. Oh, that thing? Leave it here, the silly little bug." She giggled as they drove away from the Renault. "Koitska wouldn't like you wandering around. I guess he decided to give you a job?"

"How did you know?"

She said softly, "Well, love, you're here, you know. Otherwise—never mind. What are you supposed to be doing?"

"Going to Tripler, whatever that is. In Honolulu, I guess. Then I have to build some radio equipment."

"Tripler's actually on the other side of the city. I'll take you to the gate; then you tell them where you want to go. They'll take care of it."

"I don't have any money for fare."

She laughed. After a moment she said, "Koitska's not the worst. But I'd mind my step if I were you, love. Do what he says, the best you can. You never know. You might find yourself very fortunate…"

"I already think that. I'm alive."

"Why, love, that point of view will take you far." The sports car slid smoothly to a stop at the barricade and, in the floodlights above the machine-gun nests, she looked more closely at Chandler. "What's that on your forehead, dear?"

Somehow the woolen cap had been lost. "A brand," he said shortly. "'H' for 'hoaxer.' I did something when one of you people had me, and they thought I'd done it on my own."

"Why—why, this is wonderful!" the girl said excitedly. "No wonder I thought I'd seen you before. Don't you remember? I was in the forewoman at your trial!"

CHAPTER SEVEN

A PINK and silver bus let Chandler off at Fort Street in downtown Honolulu and he walked a few blocks to the address he had been given. The name of the place was Parts 'n Plenty. He found it easily enough. It was a radio parts store; by the size of it, it had once been a big, well-stocked one; but now the counters were almost bare.

A thin-faced man with khaki-colored skin looked up and nodded. Chandler nodded back. He fingered a bin of tuning knobs, hefted a coil of two-strand antenna wire and said, "A fellow at Tripler told me to come here to pick up equipment, but I'm damned if I know what I'm supposed to do when I locate it. I don't have any money."

The dark-skinned man got up and came over to him. "Figured you for a mainlander. No sweat. Have you got a list?"

"I can make one."

"All right. Catalogues on the table behind you, if you want them." He offered Chandler a cigarette and sat against the edge of the counter, reading over Chandler's shoulder. "Ho," he said suddenly. "Koitska's square-wave generator again, right?" Chandler admitted it, and the man grinned. "Every couple months he sends somebody along. He doesn't really need the generator, you know. He just wants to see how much you know about building it, Mr.—?"

"Chandler."

"Glad to know you. I'm John Hsi. But don't go easy on the job just because it's a waste of time, Chandler; it could be pretty important to you."

Chandler absorbed the information silently and handed over his list. The man did not look at it. "Come back in about an hour," he said.

"I won't have any money in an hour, either."

"Oh, that's all right. I'll put it on Koitska's bill."

Chandler said frankly, "Look, I don't know what's going on. Suppose I came in and picked up a thousand dollars worth of stuff, would you put that on the bill, too?"

"Certainly," said Hsi optimistically. "You thinking about stealing them? What would you do with them?"

"Well…" Chandler puffed his cigarette. "Well, I could—"

"No, you couldn't. Also, it wouldn't pay, believe me," Hsi said seriously. "If there is one thing that doesn't pay, it is cheating on the Exec."

"Now, that's another good question," said Chandler. "Who is the Exec?"

Hsi shook his head. "Sorry. I don't know you, Chandler."

"You mean you're afraid even to answer a question?"

"You're damned well told I am. Probably nobody would mind what I might tell you…but 'probably' isn't good enough."

Exasperated, Chandler said, "How the devil am I supposed to know what to do next? So I take all this junk back to my room at Tripler and solder up the generator—then what?"

"Then Koitska will get in touch with you," Hsi said, not unkindly. "Play it as it comes to you, Chandler, that's the best advice I can offer." He hesitated. "Koitska's not the worst of them," he said; and then, daringly, "and maybe he's not the best, either. Just do whatever he told you. Keep on doing it until he tells you to do something else. That's all. I mean, that's all the advice I can give you. Whether it's going to be enough to satisfy Koitska is something else again."

THERE is not much to do in a strange town when you have no money. Chandler's room at what once had been Tripler General Hospital was free; the bus was free; evidently all the radio parts he could want were also free. But he did not have the price of a cup of coffee or a haircut in the pockets of the suntan slacks the deskman at Tripler had issued him. He wandered around the streets of Honolulu, waiting for the hour to be up.

At Tripler a doctor had also examined his scar and it was now concealed under a neat white bandage; he had been fed; he had bathed; he had been given new clothes. Tripler was a teeming metropolis in itself, a main building some ten stories high, a scattering of outbuildings connected to it by covered passages, with thousands of men and women busy about it. Chandler had spoken to a good many of them in the hour after waking up and before boarding the bus to Honolulu, and none of them had been free with information either.

Honolulu had not suffered greatly under the rule of the Exec. Remembering the shattered stateside cities, Chandler thought that this one had been spared nearly all the suffering of the rule of the world by the Exec, whoever they were. Dawdling down King Street, in the aromatic reek of the fish markets, Chandler could have thought himself in any port city before the grisly events of that Christmas when the planet went possessed. Crabs waved sluggishly at him from bins. Great pink-scaled fish rested on nests of ice, waiting to be sold. Smells of frying food came from half a dozen restaurants. It was only the people who were different. There was a solid sprinkling of those who, like himself, were dressed in insigneless former Army uniforms—obviously conscripts on Exec errands—and a surprising minority who, from overheard snatches of conversation, had come from countries other than the U. S. A. Russian mostly, Chandler guessed; but Russian or U. S., wearing suntans or aloha shirts, everyone he saw was marked by the visible signs of strain. There was no laughter.

Chandler saw a clock within the door of a restaurant; half an hour still to kill. He turned and wandered up, away from the water, toward the visible bulk of the hills; and in a moment he saw what made Honolulu's collective face wear its careworn frown.

It was an open square—perhaps it had once been a war memorial—and in the center of it was a fenced-off paved area where people seemed to be resting. It struck Chandler as curious that so many persons should have decided to take a nap on what surely was an uncomfortable bed of flat concrete; he approached and saw that they were not resting. Not only his eyes but his ears conveyed the message—and his nose, too, for the mild air was fetid with blood and rot. These were not sleeping men and women. Some were dead; some were unconscious; all were maimed. The pavement was slimed with their blood. None had the strength to scream, but several were moaning and even some of the unconscious ones gasped like the breathing of a man in diabetic coma. Passersby walked briskly around the metal fence, and if their glances were curious it was at Chandler they looked, not at the tortured wrecks before them. He understood that the sight of the dying men and women was familiar—was painful—and thus was ignored; it was he, himself who was the curiosity, for staring at them. He turned and fled, trying not to vomit.

HE WAS still shaken when he returned to Parts 'n Plenty.

The hour was up but Hsi shook his head. "Not yet. You can sit down over there if you like." Chandler slumped into the indicated swivel chair and stared blankly at the wall. This was far worse than anything he had seen stateside. The random terror of murders and bombs was at least a momentary thing, and when it was done it was done. This was sustained torture. He buried his head in his hands and did not look up until he heard the sound of a door opening.

Hsi, his face somehow different, was manipulating a lever on the outside of a door while a man inside, becoming visible as the door opened, was doing the same from within. It looked as though the lock on the door would not work unless both levers operated; and the man on the inside, whom Chandler had not seen before, was dressed, oddly, only in bathing trunks. His face wore the same expression as Hsi's. Chandler guessed (with practice it was becoming easy!) that both were possessed.

The man inside wheeled out two shopping carts loaded with electronic equipment of varying kinds, wordlessly received some empty ones from Hsi; and the door closed on him again.

Hsi tugged the lever down, turned, blinked and said, "All right, Chandler. Your stuff's here."

Chandler approached. "What was that all about?"

"Go to hell!" Hsi said with sudden violence. "I— Oh never mind. Sorry. But I told you already; ask somebody else your questions, not me." He gloomily began to pack the items on Chandler's list into a cardboard carton. Then he glanced at Chandler and said, apologetically, "These are tough times, buddy. I guess there's no harm in answering *some* questions. You want to know why most of my stock's locked behind an armor-plate door? Well, you ought to be able to figure that out for yourself, anyway.

The Exec doesn't like to have people playing with radios. Bert stays in the stockroom; I stay out here; twice a day the bosses open the door and we fill whatever orders they've approved. A little rough on Bert, of course. It's a ten-hour day in the stockroom for him, and nothing to do. But it could be worse. Oh, that's for sure, friend: It could be worse."

"Why the bathing suit? Hot in there?"

"Hot for Bert if they think he's smuggling stuff out," said Hsi. "You been here long enough to see the Monument yet?"

Chandler shook his head, then grimaced. "You mean up about three blocks that way? Where the people—?"

"That's right," said Hsi admiringly, "three blocks mauka from here, where the people— Where the people are serving as a very good object lesson to you and me. About a dozen there, right? Small for this time of year, Chandler. Usually there are more. Notice anything special about them?"

"They were butchered! Some of them looked like their legs had been burned right off. Their eyes had been gouged out, their faces—" Chandler brought up sharply. It had been bad enough looking at those wretched, writhing semi-cadavers; he did not want to talk about them.

The parts man nodded seriously. "Sometimes there are more, and sometimes they're worse hurt than that. Have you got any idea how they get that way? They do it to themselves, that's how. My own brother was out there for a week, last Statehood Day. He jumped feet first into a concrete mixer, and it took him seven days to die after I put him on my shoulder and carried him out there. I didn't like it, of course, but I didn't exactly have any choice; I wasn't running my own body at the time. Neither was he when he jumped. He was made to do it, because he used to have Bert's job and he thought he'd take a little short-wave set home. Like I said, you don't want to cheat on the Exec because it doesn't pay."

"But what the devil am I supposed to—"

Hsi held up his hand. "Don't ask me how to keep out of that Monument bunch, Chandler. *I* don't know. Do what you're told and don't do anything you aren't told to do; that is the whole of the law. Now do me a favor and get out of here so I can pack up these other orders." He turned his back on Chandler.

CHAPTER EIGHT

BY THE morning of the fourth day on the island of Oahu Chandler had learned enough of the ropes to have signed a money-chit at the Tripler currency office against Koitska's account.

That was about all he had learned, except for a few practical matters like where meals were served and the location of the fresh-water swimming pool at the back of the grounds. He was killing time using the pool when, in the middle of a jackknife from the ten-foot board, he felt himself seized. He sprawled into the water with a hard splashing slap, threshed about and, as he came to the surface, found himself giggling.

"Sorry, dear," he apologized to himself, "but we don't carry our weight in the same places, you know. Get that square-what'sit thingamajig, like an angel, and meet me in front by the flagpole in twenty minutes."

He recognized the voice, even if his own vocal chords had made it. It was the girl who had driven him back from the interview with Koitska, the one who had casually announced she had saved his life at his hoaxing trial. Chandler swam to the side of the pool and toweled as he trotted toward his quarters. She was from Koitska now, of course; which meant that his "test" was about to be graded.

Quickly though he dressed, she was there before him, standing beside a low-slung sports car and chatting with one of the grounds-keepers. An armful of Hawaiian leis dangled beside her, and although she wore the coronet, which was evidence of her status, the gardener did not seem to fear her. "Come along, love," she called to Chandler. "Koitska wants your thingummy. Chuck it in the trunk if it'll fit, and we'll head waikiki wikiwiki. Don't I say that nicely? But I only fool the malihinis, like you."

She chattered away as the little car dug its rear wheels into the drive and leaped around the green and out the gate.

The wind howled by them, the sun was bright, the sky was piercingly blue. Riding next to this beautiful girl, it was hard for

Chandler to remember that she was one of those who had destroyed his world. It was a terrible thing to have so much hatred and to feel it so diluted. Not even Koitska seemed a terrible enough enemy to accept such a load of detestation; it was hate without an object, and it recoiled on the hater, leaving him turgid and constrained. If he could not hate his onetime friend Jack Souther for defiling and destroying his wife, it was almost as hard to hate Souther's anonymous possessor. It could even have been Koitska. It could even have been this girl by his side. In the strange, cruel fantasies with which the Execs indulged themselves it was likely enough that they would sometimes assume the body, and the role, of the opposite sex. Why not? Strange, ruthless morality; it was impossible to evaluate it by any human standards.

It was also impossible to think of hatred with her beside him. They soared around Honolulu on a broad expressway and paralleled the beach toward Waikiki. "Look, dear. Diamond Head! Mustn't ignore it—very bad form—like not going to see the night-blooming cereus at the Punahou School. You haven't missed that, have you?"

"I'm afraid I have—"

"Rosalie. Call me Rosalie, dear."

"I'm afraid I have, Rosalie." For some reason the name sounded familiar.

"Shame, oh, shame! They say it was wonderful night before last. Looks like cactus to me, but—"

Chandler's mental processes had worked to a conclusion. "Rosalie *Pan!*" he said. "Now I know!"

"Know what? You mean—" she swerved around a motionless Buick, parked arrogantly five feet from the curb—"you mean you didn't know who I was? And to think I used to pay five thousand a year for publicity."

Chandler said, smiling, and almost relaxed, "I'm sorry, but musical comedies weren't my strong point. I did see you once, though, on television. Then, let's see, wasn't there something about you disappearing—"

She nodded, glancing at him. "There sure was, dear. I almost froze to death getting out to that airport. Of course, it was worth it, I found out later. If I hadn't been took, as they say, I would've been dead, because you remember what happened to New York about an hour later."

"You must have had some friends," Chandler began, and let it trail off. So did the girl. After a moment she began to talk about the scenery again, pointing out the brick-red and purple bougainvillea, describing how the shoreline had looked before they'd "cleaned it up." "Oh, thousands and thousands of the *homeliest* little houses. You'd have hated it. So we have done at least a few good things, anyway," she said complacently, and began gently to probe into his life story. But as they stopped before the TWA message center, a few moments later, she said, "Well, love, it's been fun. Go on in; Koitska's expecting you. I'll see you later." And her eyes added gently: *I hope.*

CHANDLER got out of the car, turned...and felt himself taken. His voice said briskly, *"Zdrestvoi, Rosie. Gd'yeh Koitska?"*

Unsurprised the girl pointed to the building. *"Kto govorit?"*

Chandler's voice answered in English, with a faint Oxford accent: "It is I, Rosie, Kalman. Where's Koitska's tinkertoy? Oh, all right, thanks; I'll just pick it up and take it in. Hope it's all right. I must say one wearies of breaking in these new fellows."

Chandler's body ambled around to the trunk of the car, took out the square-wave generator on its breadboard base and slouched into the building. It called ahead in the same language and was answered wheezily from above: Koitska. *"Zdrestvoi. Iditye suda ko mneh. Kto, Kalman?"*

"Konyekhno!" cried Chandler's voice and he was carried in and up to where the fat man lounged in a leather-upholstered wheelchair. There was a conversation, long minutes of it, while the two men poked at the generator. Chandler did not understand a word until he spoke to himself: "You—what's your name."

"Chandler," Koitska filled in.

"You, Chandler. D'you know anything at all about submillimeter microwaves? Tell Koitska." Briefly Chandler felt himself free—long enough to nod; then he was possessed again, and Koitska repeated the nod. "Good, then. Tell Koitska what experience you've had."

Again free, Chandler said, "Not a great deal of actual experience. I worked with a group at Cal tech on spectroscopic measurements in the million-megacycle range. I didn't design any of the equipment, though I helped put it together." He recited his degrees until Koitska raised a languid hand.

"*Shto*, I don't care. If ve gave you diagrams you could build?"

"Certainly, if I had the equipment. I suppose I'd need—"

But Koitska stopped him again. "I know vot you need," he said damply. "Enough. Ve see." In a moment Chandler was taken again, and his voice and Koitska's debated the matter for a while, until Koitska shrugged, turned his head and seemed to go to sleep.

Chandler marched himself out of the room and out into the driveway before his voice said to him: "You've secured a position, then. Go back to Tripler until we send for you. It'll be a few days, I expect."

And Chandler was free again.

He was also alone. The girl in the Porsche was gone. The door of the TWA building had latched itself behind him. He stared around him, swore, shrugged and circled the building to the parking lot at back, on the chance that a car might be there for him to borrow.

Luckily, there was. There were four, in fact, all with keys in them. He selected a Ford, puzzled out the likeliest road back to Honolulu and turned the key in the starter.

It was fortunate, he thought, that there had been several cars; if there had been only one he would not have dared to take it, for fear of stranding Koitska or some other exec who might easily blot him out in annoyance. He did not wish to join the wretches at the Monument.

It was astonishing how fear had become a part of his life.

The trouble with this position he had somehow secured—one of the troubles—was that there was no union delegate to settle employee grievances. Like no transportation. Like no clear idea of working hours, or duties. Like no mention at all—of course—of wages. Chandler had no idea what his rights were, if any at all, or of what the penalties would be if he overstepped them.

The maimed victims at the Monument supplied a clue, of course. He could not really believe that that sort of punishment would be applied for minor infractions. Death was so much less trouble. Even death was not really likely, he thought, for a simple lapse.

He *thought*.

He could not be sure, of course. He could be sure of only one thing: He was now a slave, completely a slave, a slave until the day he died. Back on the mainland there was the statistical likelihood of occasional slavery-by-possession, but there it was only the body that was enslaved, and only for moments. Here, in the shadow of the execs, it was all of him, forever, until death or a miracle turned him loose.

ON THE second day following, he returned to his room at Tripler after breakfast, and found a Honolulu city policeman sitting hollow-eyed on the edge of his bed. The man stood up as Chandler came in. "So," he grumbled, "you take so long! Here. Is diagrams, specs, parts lists, all. You get everything three days from now, then we begin."

The policeman, no longer Koitska, shook himself, glanced stolidly at Chandler and walked out, leaving a thick manila envelope on the pillow. On it was written, in a crabbed hand: *All secret! Do not show diagrams!*

Chandler opened the envelope and spilled its contents on the bed.

An hour later he realized that sixty minutes had passed in which he had not been afraid. It was good to be working again, he thought, and then that thought faded away again as he returned to studying the sheaves of circuit diagrams and closely typed pages of specifications. It was not only work, it was hard work, and absorbing. Chandler knew enough about the very short wavelength radio spectrum to know that the device he was supposed to build was no proficiency test; this was for real. The more he puzzled over it the less he could understand of its purpose. There was a transmitter and there was a receiver. Astonishingly, neither was directional: that ruled out radar, for example. He rejected immediately the thought that the radiation was for spectrum analysis, as in the Caltech project—unfortunate, because that was the only application with which he had first-hand familiarity; but impossible.

The thing was too complicated. Nor could it be a simple message transmitter—no, perhaps it could, assuming there was a reason for using the submillimeter bands instead of the conventional, far simpler short-wave spectrum. Could it? The submillimeter waves were line-of-sight, of course, but would ionosphere scatter make it possible for them to cover great distances? He could not remember. Or was that irrelevant, since perhaps they needed only to cover the distances between islands in their own archipelago? But then, why all the power? And in any case, what about this fantastic switching panel, hundreds of square feet of it even though it was transistorized and subminiaturized and involving at least a dozen sophisticated technical refinements he hadn't the training quite to understand? AT&T could have handled every phone call in the United States with less switching than this—in the days when telephone systems spanned a nation instead of a fraction of a city. He pushed the papers together in a pile and sat back, smoking a cigarette, trying to remember what he could of the theory behind submillimeter radiation.

At half a million megacycles and up, the domain of quantum theory began to be invaded. Rotating gas molecules, constricted to a few energy states, responded directly to the radio waves. Chandler remembered late-night bull sessions in Pasadena during which it had been pointed out that the possibilities in the field were enormous—although only possibilities, for there was no engineering way to reach them, and no clear theory to point the way—suggesting such strange ultimate practical applications as the receiverless radio, for example. Was that what he had here?

He gave up. It was a question that would burn at him until he found the answer, but just now he had work to do, and he'd better be doing it.

Skipping lunch entirely, he carefully checked the components lists, made a copy of what he would need, checked the original envelope and its contents with the man at the main receiving desk for his safe, and caught the bus to Honolulu.

At the Parts 'n Plenty store, Hsi read the list with a faint frown that turned into a puzzled scowl. When he put it down he looked at Chandler for a few moments without speaking.

"Well, Hsi? Can you get all this for me?" The parts man shrugged and nodded. "Koitska said in three days."

Hsi looked startled, then resigned. "That puts it right up to me, doesn't it? All right. Wait a moment."

He disappeared in the back of the store, where Chandler heard him talking on what was evidently an intercom system. He came back in a few minutes and slipped Chandler's list into a slit in the locked door. "Tough for Bert," he said. "He'll be working all night, getting started—but I can take it easy till tomorrow. By then he'll know what we don't have, and I'll find some way to get it." He shrugged again, but his face was lined. Chandler wondered how one went about finding, for example, a thirty-megawatt klystron tube; but it was Hsi's problem. He said:

"All right, I'll see you Monday."

"Wait a minute, Chandler." Hsi eyed him. "You don't have anything special to do, do you? Well, come have dinner with me. Maybe I can get to know you. Then maybe I can answer some of your questions, if you like."

THEY TOOK a bus out Kapiolani Boulevard, then got out and walked a few blocks to a restaurant named Mother Chee's. Hsi was well known there, it seemed. He led Chandler to a booth at the back, nodded to the waiter, ordered without looking at the menu and sat back. "You malihinis don't know much about food," he said, humorously patronizing. "I think you'll like it. It's all fish, anyway."

The man was annoying. Chandler was moved to say, "Too bad, I was hoping for duck in orange sauce, perhaps some snow peas—"

Hsi shook his head. "There's meat, all right, but not here. You'll only find it in the places where the execs sometimes go... Tell me something, Chandler. What's that scar on your forehead."

Chandler touched it, almost with surprise. Since the medics had treated it he had almost forgotten it was there. He began to explain, then paused, looking at Hsi, and changed his mind. "What's the score? You testing me, too? Want to see if I'll lie about it?"

Hsi grinned. "Sorry. I guess that's what I was doing. I do know what an 'H' stands for; we've seen them before. Not many. The ones that do get this far usually don't last long. Unless, of course, they are working for somebody whom it wouldn't do to offend," he explained.

"So what you want to know, then, is whether I was really hoaxing or not. Does it make any difference?"

"Damn right it does, man! We're slaves, but we're not animals!" Chandler had gotten to him; the parts man looked startled, then sallow, as he observed his own vehemence.

"Sorry, Hsi. It makes a difference to me, too. Well, I wasn't hoaxing. I was possessed, just like any other everyday rapist-murderer, only I couldn't prove it. And it didn't look too good for me, because the damn thing happened in a pharmaceuticals plant. That was supposed to be about the only place in town where you could be sure you wouldn't be possessed, or so everybody thought. Including me. Up to the time I went ape."

Hsi nodded. The waiter approached with their drinks. Hsi looked at him appraisingly, then did a curious thing. He gripped his left wrist with his right hand, quickly, then released it again. The waiter did not appear to notice. Expertly he served the drinks, folded small pink floral napkins, dumped and wiped their ashtray in one motion—and then, so quickly that Chandler was not quite sure he had seen it, caught Hsi's wrist in the same fleeting gesture just before he turned and walked away.

Without comment Hsi turned back to Chandler. He said, "I believe you. Would you like to know why it happened? Because I think I can tell you. The execs have all the antibiotics they need now."

"You mean—" Chandler hesitated.

"That's right. They did leave some areas alone, as long as they weren't fully stocked on everything they might want for the foreseeable future. Wouldn't you?"

"I might," Chandler said cautiously, "if I knew what I was— being an exec."

Hsi said, "Eat your dinner. I'll take a chance and tell you what I know." He swallowed his whiskey-on-the-rocks with a quick backward jerk of the head. "They're mostly Russians—you must know that much for yourself. The whole thing started in Russia."

Chandler said, "Well, that's pretty obvious. But Russia was smashed up as much as anywhere else. The whole Russian government was killed—wasn't it?"

Hsi nodded. "They're not the government. Not the exec. Communism doesn't mean any more to them than the Declaration of Independence does—which is nothing. It's very simple, Chandler: they're a project that got out of hand."

BACK four years ago, he said, in Russia, it started in the last days of the Second Stalinite Regime, before the Neo-Krushchevists took over power in the January Push.

The Western World had not known exactly what was going on, of course. The "mystery wrapped in a riddle surrounded by an enigma" had become queerer and even more opaque after Kruschchev's death and the revival of such fine old Soviet institutions as the Gay Pay Oo. That was the development called the Freeze, when the Stalinites seized control in the name of the sacred Generalissimo of the Soviet Fatherland, a mighty-missile party, dedicated to bringing about the world revolution by force of sputnik. The neo-Krushchevists, on the other hand, believed that honey caught more flies than vinegar; and, although there were few visible adherents to that philosophy during the purges of the Freeze, they were not all dead. Then, out of the Donbas Electrical Workshop, came sudden support for their point of view.

It was a weapon. It was more than a weapon, an irresistible tool—more than that, the way to end all disputes forever. It was a simple radio transmitter (Hsi said)—or so it seemed, but its frequencies were on an unusual band and its effects were remarkable. It controlled the minds of men. The "receiver" was the human brain. Through this little portable transmitter, surgically patch-wired to the brain of the person operating it, his entire personality was transmitted in a pattern of very short waves that could invade and modulate the personality of any other human being in the world. For that matter, of any animal, as long as the creature had enough "mind" to seize—

"What's the matter?" Hsi interrupted himself, staring at Chandler. Chandler had stopped eating, his hand frozen midway to his mouth. He shook his head.

"Nothing. Go on." Hsi shrugged and continued.

While the Western World was celebrating Christmas—the Christmas before the first outbreak of possession in the outside world—the man who invented the machine was secretly demonstrating it to another man. Both of them were now dead. The inventor had been a Pole, the other man a former Party leader who, four years before, had rescued the inventor's dying father from a Siberian work camp. The Party leader had reason to congratulate himself on that leaf cast on the water. There were only three working models of the transmitter—what ultimately was refined into the coronet Chandler had seen on the heads of Koitska and the girl—but that was enough for the January push.

The Stalinites were out. The neo-Krushchevists were in.

A whole factory in the Donbas was converted to manufacturing these little mental controllers as fast as they could be produced— and that was fast, for they were simple in design to begin with and were quickly refined to a few circuits. Even the surgical wiring to the brain became unnecessary as induction coils tapped the encephalic rhythms. Only the great amplifying hookup was really complicated. Only one of those was necessary, for a single amplifier could serve as rebroadcaster—modulator for thousands of the headsets.

"Are you sure you're all right?" Hsi demanded.

Chandler put down his fork, lit a cigarette and beckoned to the waiter. "I'm all right. I just want another drink."

He needed the drink. For now he knew what he was building for Koitska.

THE waiter brought two more drinks and carried away the uneaten food. "We don't know exactly who did what after that," Hsi said, "but somehow or other it got out of hand. I think it was the technical crew of the factory that took over. I suppose it was an inevitable danger." He grinned savagely. "I can just imagine the Party workers in the factory," he said, "trying to figure out how to keep them in line—bribe them or terrify them? Give them dachas or send a quota to Siberia? Neither would work, of course, because there isn't any bribe you can give to a man who only has to stretch out his hand to take over the world, and you can't frighten a man who can make you slit your own throat. Anyway, the next thing that happened—the following Christmas—was when they took over the world. It wasn't a Party movement at all any more. A lot of the workers were Czechs and Hungarians and Poles, and the first thing they wanted to do was even a few scores.

"So here they are! Before they let the whole world go bang they got out of range. They got themselves out of Russia on two Red Navy cruisers, about a thousand of them; then they systematically triggered off every ballistic missile they could find...and they could find all of them, sooner or later, it was just a matter of looking. As soon as it was safe they moved in here. Best place in the world for them.

"There are only a thousand or so of them here on the Islands, and nobody outside the Islands even knows where they are. If they did, what good would it do them? They can kill anyone, anywhere. They kill for fun, but sometimes they kill for a reason too. When one of them goes wandering for kicks he makes it a point to mess up all the transport and communications facilities he comes across—especially now, since they've stockpiled everything they're likely to need for the next twenty years. We don't know what they're planning to do when the twenty years are up. Maybe they don't care. Would you?"

Chandler drained his drink and shook his head. "One question," he said. "Who's 'we'?"

Hsi carefully unwrapped a package of cigarettes, took one out and lit it. He looked at it as though he was not enjoying it; cigarettes had a way of tasting stale these days. As they were. "Just a minute," he said.

Tardily Chandler remembered the quick grasp of the waiter's fingers on Hsi's wrist, and that the waiter had been hovering, inconspicuously close, all through their meal. Hsi was waiting for the man to return.

In a moment the waiter was back, looking directly at Chandler. He looped his own wrist with his fingers and nodded. Hsi said softly, " 'We' is the Society of Slaves. That's all of us—slaves—but only a few of us belong to the Society. We—"

There was a crash of glass. The waiter had dropped their tray.

Across the table from Chandler, Hsi looked suddenly changed. His left hand lay on the table before him, his right hand poised over it. Apparently he had been about to show Chandler again the sign he had made.

But he could not do it. His hand paused and fluttered, like a captured bird. Captured it was. Hsi was captured. Out of Hsi's mouth, with Hsi's voice, came the light, tonal rhythms of Rosalie Pan. *"This* is an unexpected pleasure, love! I never expected to see you here. Enjoying your meal?"

CHAPTER NINE

CHANDLER had his empty glass halfway to his lips, automatically, before he realized there was nothing in it to brace him. He said hoarsely, "Yes, thanks. Do you come here often?" It was like the banal talk of a language guide, wildly inappropriate to what had been going on a moment before. He was shaken.

"Oh, I love it," cooed Hsi, investigating the dishes before him. "All finished, I see. Too bad. Your friend doesn't feel like he ate much, either."

"I guess he wasn't hungry," Chandler managed.

"Well, I am." Hsi cocked his head and smiled like a female impersonator. "I know! Are you doing anything special right now, love? I know you've eaten, but well, I've been a good girl and I guess I can eat a real meal, I mean not with somebody else's teeth, and still keep the calories in line. Suppose I meet you down at the Beach? There's a place there where the luau is divine. I can be there in half an hour."

Chandler's breathing was back to normal. Why not? "I'll be delighted."

"Luigi the Wharf Rat, that's the name of it. They won't let you in, though, unless you tell them you're with me. It's special." Hsi's eye closed in Rosalie Pan's wink. "Half an hour," Hsi said, and was again himself. He began to shake.

The waiter brought him straight whiskey and, pretense abandoned, stood by while Hsi drank it. After a moment he said, "Scares you. But—I guess we're all right. She couldn't have heard much. You'd better go, Chandler. I'll talk to you again some other time."

Chandler stood up. But he couldn't leave Hsi like that. "Are you all right?"

Hsi almost managed control. "Oh—I think so. Not the first time it's come close, you know. Sooner or later it'll come closer still and that will be the end, but—yes, I'm all right for now."

Chandler tarried. "You were saying something about the Society of Slaves."

"Damn it, go!" Hsi barked. "She'll be waiting for you... Sorry, I didn't mean to shout. But go." As Chandler turned, he said more quietly, "Come around to the store tomorrow. Maybe we can finish our talk then."

LUIGI the Wharf Rat's was not actually on the beach but on the bank of a body of water called the Ala Wai Canal. Across the water were the snow-topped hills. A maitre-de escorted Chandler personally to a table on a balcony, and there he waited. Rosalie's "half-hour" was nearly two; but then he heard her calling him from across the room, in the voice which had reached a thousand second balconies, and he rose as she came near.

She said lightly, "Sorry. You ought to be flattered, though. It's a twenty-minute drive—and an hour and a half to put on my face, so you won't be ashamed to be seen with me. Well, it's good to be out in my own skin for a change. Let's eat!"

The talk with Hsi had left a mark on Chandler that not even this girl's pretty face could obscure. It was a pretty face, though, and she was obviously exerting herself to make him enjoy himself. He could not help responding to her mood.

She talked of her life on the stage, the excitement of a performance, the entertainers she had known. Her conversation was one long name-drop, but it was not pretense: the world of the famous was the world she had lived in. It was not a world that Chandler had ever visited, but he recognized the names. Rosie had been married once to an English actor whose movies Chandler had made a point of watching on television. It was interesting, in a way, to know that the man snored and lived principally on vitamin pills. But it was a view of the man that Chandler had not sought.

The restaurant drew its clientele mostly from the execs, young ones or young-acting ones, like the girl. The coronets were all over. There had been a sign on the door:

KAPU, WALIHINI!

to mark it off limits to anyone not an exec or a collaborator. Still, Chandler thought, who on the island was not a collaborator? The only effective resistance a man could make would be to kill everyone within reach and then himself, thus depriving them of slaves—and that was, after all, only what the execs themselves had done in other places often enough. It would inconvenience them only slightly. The next few planeloads or shiploads of possessed warm bodies from the mainland would be permitted to live, instead of being required to dash themselves to destruction, like the crew of the airplane that had carried Chandler. Thus the domestic stocks would be replenished.

An annoying feature of dining with Rosalie in the flesh, Chandler found, was that half a dozen times while they were talking he found himself taken, speaking words to Rosie that were not his own, usually in a language he did not understand. She took it as a matter of course. It was merely a friend, across the room or across the island, using Chandler as the casual convenience of a telephone. "Sorry," she apologized blithely after it happened for the third time, and then stopped. "You don't like that, love, do you?"

"Can you blame me?" He stopped himself from saying more; he was astonished even so at his tone.

She said it for him. "I know. It takes away your manhood, I suppose. Please don't let it do that to you, love. We're not so bad. Even—" She hesitated, and did not go on. "You know," she said, "I came here the same way you did. Kidnapped off the stage of the Winter Garden. Of course, the difference was the one who kidnapped me was an old friend. Though I didn't know it at the time and it scared me half to death."

Chandler must have looked startled. She nodded. "You've been thinking of us as another race, haven't you? Like the Neanderthals or—well, worse than that, maybe." She smiled. "We're not. About half of us came from Russia in the first place, but the others are from all over. You'd be astonished, really." She mentioned several names, world-famous scientists, musicians, writers, "Of course, not everybody can qualify for the club, love. Wouldn't be exclusive otherwise. The chief rule is loyalty. I'm loyal," she added gently after a moment, "and don't you forget it. Have to be. Whoever becomes an exec has to be with us, all the way. There are tests. It has to be that way—not only for our protection. For the world's."

Chandler was genuinely startled at that. Rosie nodded seriously. "If one exec should give away something he's not supposed to it would upset the whole applecart. There are only a thousand of us, and I guess probably two billion of you, or nearly. The result would be complete destruction."

Of the Executive Committee, Chandler thought she meant at first, but then he thought again. No. Of the world. For the thousand execs, outnumbered though they were two million to one, could not fail to triumph. The contest would not be in doubt. If the whole thousand execs at once began systematically to kill and destroy, instead of merely playing at it as the spirit moved them, they could all but end the human race overnight. A man could be made to slash his throat in a quarter of a minute. An exec, killing, killing, killing without pause, could destroy his own two million enemies in an eight-hour day.

And there were surer, faster ways. Chandler did not have to imagine them, he had seen them. The massacre of the Orphalese, the victims at the Monument—they were only crumbs of destruction. What had happened to New York City showed what mass production methods could do. No doubt there were bombs left, even if only chemical ones. Shoot, stab, crash, blow up; swallow poison, leap from window, slit throat. Every man a murderer, at the touch of a mind from Hawaii; and if no one else was near to murder, surely each man could find a victim in himself. In one ravaging day mankind would cease to exist as a major force. In a week the only survivors would be those in such far off and hopelessly impotent places that they were not worth the trouble of tracking down.

"YOU hate us, don't you?" Chandler paused and tried to find an answer. Rosie was not either belligerent or mocking. She was only sympathetically trying to reach his point of view. He shook his head silently.

"Not meaning 'no'—meaning 'no comment'? Well, I don't blame you, love. But do you see that we're not altogether a bad thing? It's bad that there should be so much violence. In a way. Hasn't there always been violence? And what were the alternatives? Until we came along the world was getting ready to kill itself anyway."

"There's a difference," Chandler mumbled. He was thinking of his wife. He and Margot had loved each other as married couples do—without any very great, searing compulsion; but with affection, with habit and with sporadic passion. Chandler had not given much thought to the whole, though he was aware of the parts, during the last years of his marriage. It was only after Margot's murder that he had come to know that the sum of those parts was a quite irreplaceable love.

But Rosie was shaking her head. "The difference is all on our side. Suppose Koitska's boss had never discovered the coronets. At any moment one country might have got nervous and touched off the whole thing—not carefully, the way we did it, with most of the really dirty missiles fused safe and others landing where they were supposed to go. I mean, touched off a *war*. The end, love. The bloody *finis*. The ones that were killed at once would have been the lucky ones. No, love," she said, in dead earnest, "we aren't the worst things that ever happened to the world. Once the—well, the *bad* part—is over, people will understand what we really are."

"And what's that, exactly?"

She hesitated, smiled and said modestly, "We're gods."

It took Chandler's breath away—not because it was untrue, but because it had never occurred to him that gods were aware of their deity.

"We're gods, love, with the privilege of electing mortals to the club. Don't judge us by anything that has gone before. Don't judge us by anything. We are a New Thing. We don't have to conform to precedent because we upset all precedents. From now on, to the end of time, the rules will grow from us."

She patted her lips briskly with a napkin and said, "Would you like to see something? Let's take a little walk."

She took him by the hand and led him across the room, out to a sundeck on the other side of the restaurant. They were looking down on what had once been a garden. There were people in it; Chandler was conscious of sounds coming from them, and he was able to see that there were dozens of them, perhaps a hundred, and that they all seemed to be wearing suntans like his own.

"From Tripler?" he guessed.

"No, love. They pick out those clothes themselves. Stand there a minute."

The girl in the coronet walked out to the rail of the sun deck, where pink and amber spotlights were playing on nothing. As she came into the colored lights there was a sigh from the people in the garden. A man walked forward with an armload of leis and deposited them on the ground below the rail.

They were *adoring* her.

Rosalie stood gravely for a moment, then nodded and returned to Chandler.

"They began doing that about a year ago," she whispered to him, as a murmur of disappointment came up from the crowd. "Their own idea. We didn't know what they wanted at first, but they weren't doing any harm. You see, love," she said softly, "we can make them do anything we like. But we don't make them do that."

HOURS later, Chandler was not sure just how, they were in a light plane flying high over the Pacific, clear out of sight of land: The moon was gold above them, the ocean black beneath.

Chandler stared down as the girl circled the plane, slipping lower toward the water, silent and perplexed. But he was not afraid. He was almost content. Rosie was good company—gay, cheerful—and she had treasures to share. It had been an impulse of hers; a long drive in her sports car and a quick, comfy flight over the ocean to cap the evening. It had been a lovely impulse. He reflected gravely that he could understand now how generations of country maidens had been dazzled and despoiled. A touch of luxury was a great seducer.

The coronet on the girl's body could catch his body at any moment. She had only to think herself into his mind, and her will, flashed to a relay station like the one he was building for Koitska, at loose in infinity, could sweep into him and make him a puppet. If she chose, he would open that door beside him and step out into a thousand feet of air and a meal for the sharks.

But he did not think she would do it. He did not think anyone would, really, though with his own eyes he had seen some anyones do things as bad as that and sickeningly worse. There was no corrupt whim of the most diseased mind in history that some torpid exec had not visited on a helpless man, woman or child in the past years. Even as they flew here, Chandler knew, the gross bodies that lay in luxury in the island's villas were surging restlessly around the world; and death and horror remained where they had passed. It was a paradox too great to be reconciled, this girl and this vileness. He could not forget it, but he could not feel it in his glands. She was pretty. She was gay. He began to think thoughts that had left him alone for a long time.

The dark bulk of the island showed ahead and they were sinking toward a landing.

The girl landed skillfully on a runway that sprang into light as she approached—electronic wizardry, or the coronet and some tethered serf at a switch? It didn't matter. Nothing mattered very greatly at that moment to Chandler.

"Thank you, love," she said, laughing. "I liked that. It's all very well to use someone else's body for this sort of thing, but every now and then I want to keep my own in practice."

She linked arms with him as they left the plane. "When I was first given the coronet here," she reminisced, amusement in her voice, "I got the habit real bad. I spent six awful months—really, six months in bed! And by myself at that. Oh, I was all over the world, and skin-diving on the Barrier Reef and skiing in Norway and—well," she said, squeezing his arm, "never *mind* what all. And then one day I got on the scales, just out of habit. Do you know what I *weighed?*" She closed her eyes in mock horror, but they were smiling when she opened them again. "I won't do that again, love. Of course, a lot of us do let ourselves go. Even Koitska. Especially Koitska. And some of the women— But just between us, the ones who do really didn't have much to keep in shape in the first place."

She led the way into a villa that smelled of jasmine and gardenias, snapped her fingers and subdued lights came on. "Like it? Oh, we've nothing but the best. What would you like to drink?"

She fixed them both tall, cold glasses and vetoed Chandler's choice of a sprawling wicker chair to sit on. "Over here, love." She patted the couch beside her. She drew up her legs, leaning against him, very soft, warm and fragrant, and said dreamily, "Let me see. What's nice? What do you like in music, love?"

"Oh...anything."

"No, no! You're supposed to say, 'Why, the original-cast album from *Hi There.*' Or anything else I starred in." She shook her head reprovingly, and the points of her coronet caught golden reflections from the lights. "But since you're obviously a man of low taste I'll have to do the whole bit myself." She touched switches at a remote control set by her end of the couch, and in a moment dreamy strings began to come from tri-aural speakers hidden around the room. It was not *Hi There.* "That's better," she said drowsily, and in a moment, "Wasn't it nice in the plane?"

"It was fine," Chandler said. Gently—but firmly—he sat up and reached automatically into his pocket.

The girl sighed and straightened. "Cigarette? They're on the table beside you. Hope you like the brand. They only keep one big factory going, not to count those terrible Russian things that're all air and no smoke." She touched his forehead with cool fingers. "You never told me about that, love."

It was like an electric shock—the touch of her fingers and the touch of reality at once. Chandler said stiffly, "My brand. But I thought you were there at the trial."

"Oh, only now and then. I missed all the naughty parts— though, to tell the truth that's why I was hanging around. I do like to hear a little naughtiness now and then…but all I heard was that stupid lawyer and that stupid judge. Made me mad." She giggled. "Lucky for you. I was so irritated I decided to spoil their fun too."

CHANDLER sat up and took a long pull at his drink. Curiously, it seemed to sober him. He said: "It's nothing. I happened to rape and kill a young girl. Happens every day. Of course, it was one of your friends that was doing it for me, but I didn't miss any of what was going on, I can give you a blow-by-blow description if you like. The people in the town where I lived, at that time, thought I was doing it on my own, though, and they didn't approve. Hoaxing—you know? They thought I was so perverse and cruel that I would do that sort of thing under my own power, instead of with some exec—or, as they would have put it, being ignorant, some imp, or devil, or demon—pulling the strings."

He was shaking. He waited for what she had to say; but she only whispered, "I'm sorry, love," and looked so contrite and honest that, as rapidly as it had come upon him, his anger passed.

He opened his mouth to say something to her. He didn't get it said. She was sitting there, looking at him, alone and soft and inviting. He kissed her; and as she returned the kiss, he kissed her again, and again.

But less than an hour later he was in her Porsche, cold sober, raging, frustrated, miserable. He slammed it through the unfamiliar gears as he sped back to the city.

She had left him. They had kissed with increasing passion, his hands playing about her, her body surging toward him, and then, just then, she whispered, "No, love." He held her tighter and without another word she opened her eyes and looked at him.

He knew what mind it was that caught him then. It was her mind. Stiffly, like wood, he released her, stood up, walked to the door and locked it behind him.

The lights in the villa went out. He stood there, boiling, looking into the shadows through the great, wide, empty window. He could see her lying there on the couch, and as he watched he saw her body toss and stir; and as surely as he had ever known anything before he knew that somewhere in the world some woman—or some man!—lay locked with a lover, violent in love, and was unable to tell the other that a third party had invaded their bed.

Chandler did not know it until he saw something glistening on his wrist, but he was weeping on the wild ride back to Honolulu in the car. Her car. Would there be trouble for his taking it? God, let there be trouble! He was in a mood for trouble. He was sick and wild with revulsion.

Worse than her use of him, a casual stimulant, an aphrodisiac touch, was that she thought what she did was right. Chandler thought of the worshipping dozens under the sundeck of the exec restaurant, and Rosalie's gracious benediction as they made her their floral offerings. Blind, pathetic fools!

Not only the deluded men and women in the garden were worshippers trapped in a vile religion, he thought. It was worse. The gods and goddesses worshipped at their own divinity as well!

CHAPTER TEN

THREE days later Koitska's voice, coming from Chandler's lips, summoned him out to the TWA shack again.

Wise now in the ways of this world, Chandler commandeered a police car and was hurried out to the South Gate, where the guards allowed him a car of his own. The door of the building was unlocked and Chandler went right up.

He was astonished. The fat man was actually sitting up. He was fully dressed—more or less; incongruously he wore flowered shorts and a bright red, short-sleeve shirt, with rope sandals. He said, "You fly a *gilikopter?* No? No difference. Help me." An arm like a mountain went over Chandler's shoulders. The man must have weighed three hundred pounds. Slowly, wheezing, he limped toward the back of the room and touched a button.

A door opened.

Chandler had not known before that there was an elevator in the building. That was one of the things the exec did not consider important for his slaves to know. It lowered them with great grace and delicacy to the first floor, where a large old Cadillac, ancient but immaculately kept, the kind that used to be called a "gangster's car," waited in a private parking bay.

Chandler followed Koitska's directions and drove to an airfield where a small, Plexiglass-nosed helicopter waited. More by the force of Chandler pushing him from behind than through his own fat thighs, Koitska puffed up the little staircase into the cabin.

Illustrated by RITTER

Originally the 'copter had been fitted for four passengers. Now there was the pilot's seat and a seat beside it, and in the back a wide, soft couch. Koitska collapsed onto it. His face blanked out—he was, Chandler knew, somewhere else, just then.

In a moment his eyes opened again. He looked at Chandler with no interest at all, and turned his face to the wall.

After a moment he wheezed.

"Sit down. At de controls." He breathed noisily for a while. Then, "It von't pay you to be interested in Rosalie," he said.

Chandler was startled. He craned around in the seat but saw only Koitska's back. "I'm not! Or anyway—" But he had no place to go in that sentence, and in any case Koitska no longer seemed interested.

After a moment Koitska stirred, settled himself more comfortably, and Chandler felt himself taken. He turned to face the split wheel and the unfamiliar pedals and watched himself work the controls. It was an admirable performance. Whoever Chandler was just then—he could not guess—he was a first-class helicopter pilot.

THEY crossed a wide body of ocean and approached another island; from one quick glance at a navigation map that his eyes had taken, Chandler guessed it to be Hilo. He landed the craft expertly on the margin of a small airstrip, where two DC-3s were already parked and being unloaded, and felt himself free again.

Two husky young men, apparently native Hawaiians by their size, rolled up a ramp and assisted Koitska down it and into a building, Chandler was left to his own devices. The building was rundown but sound. Around it stalky grass clumped, long uncut, and a few mauve and scarlet blossoms, almost hidden, showed where someone had once tended beds of bougainvillea and poinsettias. He could not guess what the building had been doing there, looking like a small office-factory combination out in the remote wilds, until he caught sight of a sign the winds had blown against a wall: *Dole.* Apparently this had been headquarters for one of the plantations. Now it was stripped almost clean inside, a welter of desks and rusted machines piled heedlessly where there once had been a parking lot. New equipment was being loaded into it from the cargo planes. Chandler recognized some of it as from the list he had given the parts man, Hsi. There also seemed to be a gasoline-driven generator—a large one—but what the other things were he could not guess.

Besides Koitska, there were at least five coronet-wearing execs visible around the place. Chandler was not surprised. It would have to be something big to winkle these torpid slugs out of their shells, but he knew what it was, and that it was big enough to them indeed; in fact, it was their lives. He deduced that Koitska's plans for his future comfort required a standby transmitter to service the coronets, in case something went wrong. And clearly it was this that they were to put together here.

For ten hours, while the afternoon became dark night, they worked at a furious pace. When the sun set one of the execs gestured and the generator was started, rocking on its rubber-tired wheels as its rotors spun and fumes chugged out, and they worked on by strings of incandescent lights. It was pick-and-shovel work for Chandler, no engineering, just unloading and roughly grouping the equipment where it was ready to be assembled. The execs did not take part in the work. Nor were they idle. They busied themselves in one room of the building with some small device—Chandler could not see what—and when he looked again it was gone. He did not see them take it away and did not know where it was taken. Toward midnight he suddenly realized that it was likely some essential part that they would not permit anyone but themselves to handle, and that, no doubt, was why they had come in person, instead of working through proxies.

Just before they left Koitska and two or three of the other execs quizzed him briefly. He was too tired to think beyond the questions, but they seemed to be trying to find out if he was able to do the simpler parts of the construction without supervision, and they seemed satisfied with the answers. He flew the helicopter home, with someone else guiding his arms and legs, but he was half asleep as he did it, and he never quite remembered how he managed to get back to his room at Tripler.

THE next morning he went back to Parts 'n Plenty with an additional list, covering replacement of some parts that had been damaged. Hsi glanced at it quickly and nodded. "All this stuff I have. You can pick it up this afternoon if you like."

Chandler offered him a cigarette out of a stale pack. "About the other night—"

Hsi began to perspire, but he said, casually enough, "Interested in baseball?"

"Baseball?"

Hsi said, as though there had been nothing incongruous about the question, "There'll be a Little League game this afternoon. Back of the school on Punahou and Wilder. I thought I might stop by, then we can come back and pick up the rest of your gear. Two o'clock. Hope I'll see you."

Chandler walked away thoughtfully. He had no real intention of going there, but something in Hsi's attitude suggested more than a ball game; after a quick and poor lunch he decided to go.

The field was a dirty playground, scuffed out of what had probably once been an attractive campus. The players were ten-year-olds, of the mixture of hair colors and complexions typical of the islands. Chandler was puzzled. Surely even the wildest baseball rooter wouldn't go far out of his way for this, and yet there was an audience of at least fifty adults watching the game. And none seemed to be related to the ballplayers. The Little Leaguers played grave, careful ball, and the audience watched them without a word of parental encouragement or joy.

Hsi approached him from the shadow of the school building. "Glad you could make it, Chandler. No, no questions. Just watch."

In the fifth inning, with the score aggregating around thirty, there was an interruption. A tall, redheaded man glanced at his watch, licked his lips, took a deep breath and walked out onto the diamond. He glanced at the crowd, while the kids suspended play without surprise. Then the redheaded man nodded to the umpire and stepped off the field. The ballplayers resumed their game, but now the whole attention of the audience was on the redheaded man.

Suspicion crossed Chandler's mind. In a moment it was confirmed, as the red-headed man raised his hands waist high and clasped his right hand around his left wrist—only for a moment, but that was enough.

The ball game was a cover. Chandler was present at a meeting of what Hsi had called The Society of Slaves, the underground that dared to pit itself against the execs.

Hsi cleared his throat and said, "This is the one. I vouch for him." And that was startling too, Chandler thought, because all these wrist-circled men and women were looking at *him*.

"ALL right," said the redheaded man nervously, "let's get started then. First thing, anybody got any weapons? Sure? Take a look—we don't want any slipups. Turn out your pockets."

There was a flurry and a woman near Chandler held up a key ring with a tiny knife on it. "Penknife? Hell, yes; get rid of it. Throw it in the outfield. You can pick it up after the meeting." A hundred eyes watched the pearly object fly. "We ought to be all right here," said the redheaded man. "The kids have been playing every day this week and nobody looked in. But *watch your neighbor*. See anything suspicious, don't wait. Don't take a chance. Holler 'Kill the umpire!' or anything you like, but holler. Good and loud." He paused, breathing hard. "All right, Hsi. Introduce him."

The parts man took Chandler firmly by the shoulder. "This fellow has something for us," he said. "He's working for the exec Koitska, building what can't be anything else but a duplicate of the machine that they use to control us. He—"

"Wait a minute!" A bearded man came forward and peered furiously into Chandler's face. "Look at his head! Don't you see he's branded?"

Chandler touched his scar as the man with the beard hissed, "Damned hoaxer! This is the lowest species of life on the face of the earth—someone who pretended to be possessed in order to do some damned dirty act. What was it, hoaxer? Murder? Burning babies alive?"

Hsi economically let go of Chandler's shoulder, half turned the bearded man with one hand and swung with the other. "Shut up, Linton. Wait till you hear what he's got for us."

The bearded man, sprawling and groggy, slowly rose as Hsi explained tersely what he had guessed of Chandler's work—as much as Chandler himself knew, it seemed. "Maybe this is only a duplicate. Maybe it won't be used. But maybe it will—and Chandler's the man who can sabotage it! How would you like that? The execs switching over to this equipment while the other one is down for maintenance—and their headsets don't work!"

There was a terrible silence, except for the sounds of the children playing ball. Two runs had just scored. Chandler recognized the silence. It was hope.

Linton broke it, his blue eyes gleaming above the beard. "No! Better than that. Why wait? We can use this fellow's machine. Set it up, get us some headsets—and we can control the execs themselves!"

THE silence was even longer; then there was a babble of discussion, but Chandler did not take part in it. He was thinking. It was a tremendous thought.

Suppose a man like himself were actually able to do what they wanted of him. Never mind the practical difficulties—learning how it worked, getting a headset, bypassing the traps Koitska would surely have set to prevent just that. Never mind the penalties for failure. Suppose he could make it work, and find fifty headsets, and fit them to the fifty men and women here in this clandestine meeting of the Society of Slaves...

Would there, after all, be any change worth mentioning in the state of the world?

Or was Lord Acton, always and everywhere, right? Power corrupts. Absolute power corrupts absolutely. The power locked in the coronets of the exec was more than flesh and blood could stand; he could almost sense the rot in those near him at the mere thought.

But Hsi was throwing cold water on the idea. "Sorry, but I know that much: One exec can't control another. The headpieces insulate against control. Well." He glanced at his watch. "We agreed on twenty minutes maximum for this meeting," he reminded the redheaded man, who nodded.

"You're right." He glanced around the group. "I'll make the rest of it fast. News: You all know they got some more of us last week. Have you all been by the Monument? Three of our comrades were still there this morning. But I don't think they know we're organized, they think it's only individual acts of sabotage. In case any of you don't know, the execs can't read our minds. Not even when they're controlling us. Proof is we're all still alive. Hanrahan knew practically everyone of us, and he's been lying out there for a week with a broken back, ever since they caught him trying to blow up the guard pits at East Gate. They had plenty of chance to pump him if they could. *They can't*. Next thing. No more individual attacks on one exec. Not unless it's a matter of life and death, and even then you're wasting your time unless you've got a gun. They can grab your mind faster than you can cut a throat. Third thing: Don't get the idea there are good execs and bad execs. Once they put that thing on their heads they're all the same. Fourth thing. You can't make deals. They aren't that worried. So if anybody's thinking of selling out—I'm not saying anyone is—forget it." He looked around. "Anything else?"

"What about germ warfare in the water?" somebody asked.

"Still looking into it. No report yet. All right, that's enough for now. Meeting's adjourned. Watch the ball game for a while, then drift away. *One at a time.*"

Hsi was the first to go, then a couple of women together, then a sprinkling of other men. Chandler was in no particular hurry, although it seemed time to leave anyway, because the ball game appeared to be over. A ten-year-old with freckles on his face was at the plate, but he was leaning on his bat, staring at Chandler with wide, serious eyes.

Chandler felt a sudden chill. He turned, began to walk away—and felt himself seized.

HE WALKED slowly into the schoolhouse, unable to look around. Behind him he heard a confused sob, tears and a child's voice trying to blubber through:

"Something *funny* happened."

If the child had been an adult it might have been warning enough. But the child had never experienced possession before, was not sure enough, was clear into the schoolhouse before the remaining members of the Society of Slaves awoke to their danger.

191

He heard a quick cry of *They got him!* Then Chandler's legs stopped walking and he addressed himself savagely. A few yards away a stout Chinese lady was mopping the tiles; she looked up at him, startled, but no more startled than Chandler was himself. "You idiot!" Chandler blazed. "Why do you get mixed up in this? Don't you know it's wrong, love? Stay here!" Chandler directed himself. "Don't you *dare* leave this building!"

And he was free again, but there was a sudden burst of screams from outside.

Bewildered, Chandler stood for a moment, as little able to move as though the girl still had him under control. Then he leaped through a classroom to a window, staring. Outside in the playground there was wild confusion. Half the spectators were on the ground, trying to rise. As he watched, a teen-age boy hurled himself at an elderly lady, the two of them falling. Another man flung himself to the ground. A woman swung her pocketbook into the face of the man next to her. One of the fallen ones rose, only to trip himself again. It was a mad spectacle, but Chandler understood it: What he was watching was a single member of the exec trying to keep a group of twenty ordinary, unarmed human beings in line. The exec was leaping from mind to mind; even so, the crowd was beginning to scatter.

Without thought Chandler started to leap out to help them; but the possessor had anticipated that. He was caught at the door. He whirled and ran toward the woman with the mop; as he was released, the woman flung herself upon him, knocking him down.

By the time he was able to get up again it was far too late to help...if there ever had been a time when he could have been of any real help.

He heard shots. Two policeman had come running into the playground, with guns drawn.

The exec who had looked at him out of the boy's eyes, who had penetrated this nest of enemies and extricated Chandler from it, had taken first things first. Help had been summoned. Quick as the coronets worked, it was no time at all until the nearest persons with weapons were located, commandeered and in action.

Two minutes later there no longer was resistance.

Obviously more execs had come to help, attracted by the commotion perhaps, or summoned at some stolen moment after the meeting had first been invaded. There were only five survivors on the field. Each was clearly controlled. They rose and stood patiently while the two police shot them, shot them, paused to reload and shot again. The last to die was the bearded man, Linton, and as he fell his eyes brushed Chandler's.

Chandler leaned against a wall.

It had been a terrible sight.

The nearness of his own death had been almost the least of it.

He had no doubt of the identity of the exec who had saved him and destroyed the others. Though he had heard the voice only as it came from his own mouth, he could not miss it. It was Rosalie Pan.

He looked out at the redheaded man, sprawled across the foul line behind third base, and remembered what he had said. There weren't any good execs or bad execs. There were only execs.

CHAPTER ELEVEN

WHATEVER Chandler's life might be worth, he knew he had given it away and the girl had given it back to him.

He did not see her for several days, but the morning after the massacre he woke to find a note beside his bed table. No one had been in the room. It was his own sleeping hand that had written it, though the girl's mind had moved his fingers:

If you get mixed up in anything like that again I won't be able to help you.
So don't! Those people are just using you, you know.
Don't throwaway your chances.
Do you like surfboarding?

Rosie

But by then there was no time for surfboarding, or for anything else but work. The construction job on Hilo had begun, and it was a nightmare. He was flown to the island with the last load of parts. No execs were present in the flesh, but in the first day Chandler lost count of how many different minds possessed his own. He began to be able to recognize them by a limp as he walked, by tags of German as he spoke, by a stutter, a distinctive gesture of annoyance, an expletive. As he was a trained engineer he was left to labor by himself for hours on end. It was worse for the others. There seemed to be a dozen execs hovering invisible around all the time; no sooner was a worker released by one than he was seized by another. The work progressed rapidly, but at the cost of utter exhaustion. By the end of the fourth day Chandler had eaten only two meals and could not remember when he had slept last. He found himself staggering when free, and furious with the fatigue-clumsiness of his own body when possessed. At sundown on the fourth day he found himself free for a moment and, incredibly, without work of his own to do just then, until someone else completed a job of patch wiring. He stumbled out into the open air and had time only to gaze around for a moment before his eyes began to close. This must once have been a lovely island. Even unkempt as it was, the trees were tall and beautiful. Beyond them a wisp of smoke was pale against the dark-blue evening sky; the breeze was scented... He woke and found he was already back in the building, reaching for his soldering gun.

There came a point at which even the will of the execs was unable to drive the flogged bodies farther, and then they were permitted to sleep for a few hours. At daybreak they were awake again. The sleep was not enough. The bodies were slow and inaccurate. Two of the Hawaiians, straining a hundred-pound component into place, staggered, slipped—and dropped it.

Appalled, Chandler waited for them to kill themselves.

But it seemed that the execs were tiring too. One of the Hawaiians said irritably, with an accent Chandler did not recognize: "That's pau. All right, you morons, you've won yourselves a vacation; we'll have to fly you in replacements. Take the day off." And incredibly all eleven of the haggard wrecks stumbling around the building were free at once.

The first thought of every man was to eat, to relieve himself, to remove a shoe and ease a blistered foot—to do any of the things they had not been permitted to do. The second thought was sleep.

Chandler dropped off at once, but he was overtired; he slept fitfully, and after an hour or two of turning on the hard ground sat up, blinking red-eyed around. He had been slow. The cushioned seats in the aircraft and cars were already taken. He stood up, stretched, scratched himself and wondered what to do next, and he remembered the thread of smoke he had seen—when? three nights ago?—against the evening sky.

In all those hours he had not had time to think one obvious thought: There should have been no smoke there! The island was supposed to be deserted.

He stood up, looked around to get his bearings, and started off in the direction he remembered.

IT WAS good to own his body, again, in poor condition as it was. It was delicious to be allowed to think consecutive thoughts.

The chemistry of the human animal is such that it heals whatever thrusts it may receive from the outside world. Short of death, its only incapacitating wound comes from itself; from the outside it can survive astonishing blows, rise again and flourish. Chandler was not flourishing, but he had begun to rise.

Time had been so compressed and blurred in the days since the slaughter at the Punahou School that he had not had time to grieve over the deaths of his briefly-met friends, or even to think of their quixotic plans against the execs. Now he began to wonder.

He understood with what thrill of hope he had been received— a man like themselves, not an exec, whose touch was at the very center of the exec power. But how firm was that touch? Was there really anything he could do?

It seemed not. He barely understood the mechanics of what he was doing, far less the theory behind it. Conceivably knowing where this installation was he could somehow get back to it when it was completed. In theory it might be that there was a way to dispense with the headsets and exert power from the big board itself.

A Cro-Magnard at the controls of a nuclear-laden jet bomber could destroy a city. Nothing stopped him. Nothing but his own invincible ignorance. Chandler was that Cro-Magnard; certainly power was here to grasp, but he had no way of knowing how to pick it up.

Still—where there was life there was hope. He decided he was wasting time that would not come again. He had been wandering along a road that led into a small town, quite deserted, but this was no time for wandering. His place was back at the installation, studying, scheming, trying to understand all he could. He began to turn, and stopped.

"Great God," he said softly, looking at what he had just seen. The town was deserted of life, but not of death.

THERE were bodies everywhere.

They were long dead, perhaps years. They seemed natural and right as they lay there. It was not surprising they had escaped his notice at first. Little was left but bones and an occasional desiccated leathery rag that might have been a face. The clothing was faded and rotted away; but enough was left of the bodies and the clothes to make it clear that none of these people had died natural deaths. A rusted blade in a chest cage showed where a knife had pierced a heart; a small skull near his feet (with a scrap of faded blue rompers near it) was shattered. On a flagstone terrace a family group of bones lay radiating outward, like a rosette. Something had exploded there and caught them all as they turned to flee. There was a woman's face, grained like oak and eyeless, visible between the fender of a truck and a crushed-in wall.

Like exhumed Pompeii, the tragedy was so ancient that it aroused only wonder. The whole town had been blotted out.

The execs did not take chances; apparently they had sterilized the whole island—probably had sterilized all of them except Oahu itself, to make certain that their isolation was complete, except for the captive stock allowed to breed and serve them in and around Honolulu.

Chandler prowled the town for a quarter of an hour, but one street was like another. The bodies did not seem to have been disturbed even by animals, but perhaps there were none big enough to show traces of such work.

Something moved in a doorway.

Chandler thought at once of the smoke he had seen, but no one answered his call and, though he searched, he could neither see nor hear anything alive.

The search was a waste of time. It also wasted his best chance to study the thing he was building. As he returned to the cinder-block structure at the end of the airstrip he heard motors and looked up to see a plane circling in for a landing.

He knew that he had only a few minutes. He spent those minutes as thriftily as he could, but long before he could even grasp the circuitry of the parts he had not himself worked on he felt a touch at his mind. The plane was rolling to a stop. He and all of them hurried over to begin unloading it.

The plane was stopped with one wingtip almost touching the building, heading directly into it—convenient for unloading, but a foolish nuisance when it came time to turn it and take off again, Chandler's mind thought while his body lugged cartons out of the plane.

But he knew the answer to that. Takeoff would be no problem, any more than it would for the other small transports at the far end of the strip.

These planes were not going to return, ever.

THE work went on, and then it was done, or all but, and Chandler knew no more about it than when it was begun. The last little bit was a careful check of line voltages and a balancing of biases. Chandler could help only up to a point, and then two execs, working through the bodies of one of the Hawaiians and the pilot of a Piper Tri-Pacer who had flown in some last-minute test equipment—and remained as part of the labor pool—laboriously worked on the final tests.

Spent, the other men flopped to the ground, waiting.

They were far gone. All of them, Chandler as much as the others. But one of them rolled over, grinned tightly at Chandler and said, "It's been fun. My name's Bradley. I always think people ought to know each other's names in cases like this. Imagine sharing a grave with some utter stranger!"

"Grave?"

Bradley nodded. "Like Pharaoh's slaves. The pyramid is just about finished, friend. You don't know what I'm talking about?" He sat up, plucked a blade of stemmy grass and put it between his teeth. "I guess you haven't seen the corpses in the woods."

Chandler said, "I found a town half a mile or so over there, nothing in it but skeletons."

"No, heavens, nothing that ancient. These are nice fresh corpses, out behind the junkheap there. Well, not *fresh*. They're a couple of weeks old. I thought it was neat of the execs to dispose of the used-up labor out of sight of the rest of us. So much better for morale...until Juan Simoa and I went back looking for a plain, simple electrical extension cord and found them."

With icy calm Chandler realized that the man was talking sense. Used-up labor: the men who had unloaded the first planes, no doubt—worked until they dropped, then efficiently disposed of, as they were so cheap a commodity that they were not worth the trouble of hauling back to Honolulu for salvage. "I see," he said. "Besides, dead men tell no tales."

"*And* spread no disease. Probably that's why they did their killing back in the tall trees. Always the chance some exec might have to come down here to inspect in person. Rotting corpses just aren't sanitary." Bradley grinned again. "I used to be a doctor at Molokai."

"Lep—" began Chandler, but the doctor shook his head.

"No, no, never say 'leprosy.' It's 'Hansen's disease.' Whatever it is, the execs were sure scared of it. They wiped out every patient we had, except a couple who got away by swimming; then for good measure they wiped out most of the medical staff too, except for a couple like me who were off-island and had the sense to keep quiet about where they'd worked. I used to," he said, rolling over his back and putting his hands behind his head, "work on pest-control for the Public Health Service in the old days. We sure knocked off a lot of rats and fleas. I never thought I'd be one of them." He was silent.

Chandler admired his courage very much. The man had fallen asleep.

Chandler looked at the others. "You going to let them kill us without a struggle?" he demanded.

The remaining Hawaiian was the only one to answer. He said, "You just don't know how much *pilikia* you're in. It isn't what we *let* them do."

"We'll see," Chandler promised grimly. "They're only human. I haven't given up yet."

BUT in the end he could not save himself; it was the girl who did. That night Chandler tossed in troubled sleep, and woke to find himself standing, walking toward the Tri-Pacer. The sun was just beginning to pink the sky and no one else was moving. "Sorry, love," he apologized to himself. "You probably need to bathe and shave, but I don't know how. Shave, I mean." He giggled. "Anyway, you'll find everything you need at my house."

He climbed into the plane.

"Ever fly before?" he asked himself. "Well, you'll love it. Here we go. *Close* the door...*snap* the belt...*turn* the switch." He admired the practiced ease with which his body started the motor, raced it with a critical eye on the instruments, turned the plane and lifted it off, up, into the rising sun.

"Oh, dear. You *do* need a bath," he told himself, wrinkling his nose humorously. "No harm. I've the nicest tub—pink, deep— and nine kinds of bath salts. But I wish you weren't so tired, love, because it's a long flight and you're wearing me out." He was silent as he bent to the correct compass heading and cranked a handle over his head to adjust the trim. "Koitska's going to be so *huhu*," he said, smiling. "Never fear, love, I can calm him down. But it's easier to do with you in one piece, you know, the other way's too late."

He was silent for a long time, then his voice began to sing.

They were songs from Rosalie's own musical comedies. Even with so poor an instrument as Chandler's voice to work with, she sang well enough to keep both of them entertained while his body brought the plane in for a landing; and so Chandler went to live in the villa that belonged to Rosalie Pan.

CHAPTER TWELVE

"LOVE," she said, "there are worse things in the world than keeping me amused when I'm not busy. We'll go to the beach again one day soon, I promise." And she was gone again.

Chandler was a concubine—not even that; he was a male geisha, convenient to play gin rummy with, or for company on the surfboards, or to make a drink.

He did not quite know what to make of himself. In bad times one hopes for survival. He had hoped; and now he had survival, perfumed and cushioned, but on what mad terms! Rosalie was a pretty girl, and a good-humored one. She was right. There were worse things in the world than being her companion; but Chandler could not adjust himself to the role.

It angered him when she got up from the garden swing and locked herself in her room—for he knew that she was not sleeping as she lay there, though her eyes were closed and she was motionless. It infuriated him when she casually usurped his body to bring an ashtray to her side, or to stop him when his hands presumed. And it drove him nearly wild to be a puppet with her friends working his strings.

He was that most of all. One exec who wished to communicate with another cast about for an available human proxy nearby. Chandler was that for Rosie Pan: her telephone, her social secretary, and on occasion he was the garment her dates put on. For Rosalie was one of the few execs who cared to conduct any major part of her life in her own skin. She liked dancing. She enjoyed dining out. It was her pleasure to display herself to the worshippers at Luigi the Wharf Rat's and to speed down the long combers on a surfboard. When another exec chose to accompany her it was Chandler's body that gave the remote "date" flesh.

He ate very well indeed—in surprising variety. He drank heavily sometimes and abstained others. Once, in the person of a Moroccan exec, he smoked an opium pipe; once he dined on roasted puppy. He saw many interesting things and, when Rosalie was occupied without him, he had the run of her house, her music library, her pantry and her books. He was not mistreated. He was pampered and praised, and every night she kissed him before she retired to her own room with the snap-lock on the door.

He was miserable.

He prowled the house in the nights after she had left him, unable to sleep. It had been bad enough on Hilo, under the hanging threat of death. But then, though he was only a slave, he was working at something that used his skill and training.

Now? Now a Pekingese could do nearly all she wanted of him. He despised in himself the knowledge that with a Pekingese's cunning he was contriving to make himself indispensable to her— her slippers fetched in his teeth, his silky mane by her hand to stroke—if not these things in actuality, then their very near equivalents.

But what else was there for him?

There was nothing. She had spared his life from Koitska, and if he offended her Koitska's sentence would be carried out.

Even dying might be better than this, he thought.

Indeed, it might be better even to go back to Honolulu and life.

IN THE morning he woke to find himself climbing the wide, carpeted steps to her room. She was not asleep; it was her mind that was guiding him.

He opened the door. She lay with a feathery coverlet pulled up to her chin, eyes open, head propped on three pillows; as she looked at him he was free. "Something the matter, love? You fell asleep sitting up."

"Sorry." She would not be put off. She made him tell her his resentments. She was very understanding and sure as she said, "You're not a dog, love. I won't have you thinking that way. You're my friend. Don't you think I need a friend?" She leaned forward. Her nightgown was very sheer; but Chandler had tasted that trap before and he averted his eyes. "You think it's all fun for us. Right? Tell me, if you thought I was doing important work— oh, *crucial* work, love—would you feel a little easier? Because I am. We've got the whole work of the island to do, and I do my share. We've got plans to make and a future to provide for. There are so few of us. One H-bomb kills us all. Don't you think it's work, keeping that bomb from ever coming here? There's all Honolulu to monitor, for they know about us there. We can't like some disgusting nitwits like your Society of Slaves destroy *us*. There's the problems of the world to see to. Why," she said with pride, "we've solved the whole Indian-Pakistani population problem in the last two months. They'll not have to worry about famine again for a dozen generations! We're working on China now; next Japan; next—oh, all the world. We'll have three-quarters of the lumps gone soon, and the rest will have space to breathe in. It's work!"

She saw his expression and said earnestly, "Don't think that! You call it murder—which it is—but it's the surgeon's knife. We're quicker and less painful than starvation, love...and if some of us enjoy the work of weeding out the unfit, does that change anything? It does not! I admit some of us are, well, *mean*. But not all. And we're improving. The new people we take in are better than the old."

She looked at him thoughtfully for a moment.

Then she shook her head. "Never mind," she said—apparently to herself. "Forget it, love. Go like an angel and fetch us both some coffee."

LIKE AN angel he went...not, he thought bitterly, like a man.

She was keeping something from him, and he was too stubborn to let her tease him out of his mood. "Everything's a secret," he complained, and she patted his cheek.

"It has to be that way." She was quite serious. "This is the biggest thing in the world. I'm fond of you, love, but I can't let that interfere with my duty."

"*Shto, Rosie?*" said Chandler's mouth thickly.

"Oh, there you are, Andrei," she said, and spoke quickly in Russian.

Chandler's brows knotted in a scowl and he barked: "*Nyeh mozhet bit!*"

"Andrei..." she said gently. "*Ya vas sprashnivayoo...*"

"*Nyet!*"

"*No Andrei...*"

Rumble, grumble; Chandler's body twitched and fumed. He heard his own name in the argument, but what the subject matter was he could not tell. Rosalie was coaxing; Koitska was refusing. But he was weakening. After minutes Chandler's shoulders shrugged; he nodded; and he was free.

"Have some more coffee, love," said Rosalie Pan with an air of triumph.

Chandler waited. He did not understand what was going on. It was up to her to enlighten him, and finally she smiled and said: "Perhaps you can join us, love. Don't say yes or no. It isn't up to you…and besides you can't know whether you want it or not until you try. So be patient a moment."

Chandler frowned; then felt his body taken. His lips barked: *"Khorashaw!"* His body got up and walked to the wall of Rosalie's room. A picture on the wall moved aside and there was a safe. Flick, flick, Chandler's own fingers dialed a combination so rapidly that he could not follow it. The door of the safe opened.

And Chandler was free, and Rosalie excitedly leaping out of the bed behind him, careless of the wisp of nylon that was her only garment, crowding softly, warmly past him to reach inside the safe. She lifted out a coronet very like her own.

She paused and looked at Chandler.

"You can't do anything to harm us with this one, love," she warned. "Do you understand that? I mean, don't get the idea that you can tell anyone anything. Or do something violent. You can't. I'll be right with you, and Koitska will be monitoring the transmitter." She handed him the coronet. "Now, when you see something interesting, you move right in. You'll see how. It's the easiest thing in the world, and— Oh, here. Put it on."

Chandler swallowed with difficulty.

She was offering him the tool that had given the execs the world. A blunter, weaker tool than her own, no doubt. But still it was power beyond his imagining. He stood there frozen as she slipped it on his head. Sprung electrodes pressed gently against his temples and behind his ears. She touched something…

Chandler stood motionless for a moment and then, without effort, floated free of his own body.

FLOATING. Floating; a jellyfish floating. Trailing tentacles that whipped and curled, floating over the sand-bound claws and chitin that clashed beneath, floating over the world's people, and them not even knowing, not even seeing…

Chandler floated.

He was up, out and away. He was drifting. Around him was no-color. He saw nothing of space or size, he only saw, or did not see but felt—smelled—tasted people. They were the sand-bound. They were the creatures that crawled and struggled below, and his tentacles lashed out at them.

Beside him floated another. The girl? It had a shape, but not a human shape—a pair of great projecting spheres, a cinctured area-rule shape. Female. Yes, undoubtedly the girl. It waved a member at him and he understood he was beckoned. He followed.

Two of sand-bound ones were ahead.

The female shape slipped into one, he into the other. It was as easy to invest this form with his own will as it was to command the muscles of his hand. They looked at each other out of sand-bound eyes. "You're a boy!" Chandler laughed. The girl laughed: "You're an old washerwoman!" They were in a kitchen where fish simmered on an electric stove. The boy-Rosie wrinkled his-her nose, blinked and was empty. Only the small almond-eyed boy was left, and he began to cry convulsively. Chandler understood. He floated out after her.

This way, this way, she gestured. A crowd of mud-bound figures. She slipped into one, he into another. They were in a bus now, rocking along an inland road, all men, all roughly dressed. Laborers going to clear a new section of Oahu of its split-level debris, Chandler thought, and looked for the girl in one of the men's eyes, could not find her, hesitated and—floated. She was hovering impatiently. This way!

He followed, and followed. They were a hundred people doing a hundred things. They lingered a few moments as a teen-age couple holding hands in the twilight of the beach. They fled from a room where Chandler was an old woman dying on a bed, and Rosalie a stolid, uncaring nurse beside her. They played follow-the-leader through the audience of a Honolulu movie theater, and sought each other, laughing, among the fish stalls of King Street. Then Chandler turned to Rosalie to speak and...it all went out...the scene disappeared...he opened his eyes, and he was back in his own flesh.

He was lying on the pastel pile rug in Rosalie's bedroom.

He got up, rubbing the side of his face. He had tumbled, it seemed. Rosalie was lying on the bed.

In a moment she opened her eyes.

"Well, love?"

He said hoarsely, "What made it stop?"

She shrugged. "Koitska turned you off. Tired of monitoring us, I expect—it's been an hour. I'm surprised his patience lasted this long."

She stretched luxuriously, but he was too full of what had happened even to see the white grace of her body. "Did you like it, love? Would you like to have it forever?"

CHAPTER THIRTEEN

FOR NINE days Chandler's status remained in limbo. He spent that day in a state of numb bemusement, remembering the men and women he had worn like garments, appalled and exhilarated. He did not see Rosalie again that day, she kept to her room and he locked out. He was still a lapdog, but a lapdog with a dream dangling before him. He went to sleep that night thinking that he was a dog who might become a god, and he had eight days left.

The next day Rosalie wheedled another hour of the coronet from Koitska. They explored the ice caves on Mount Rainier in the bodies of two sick, starving hermits and wandered arm in arm near the destroyed International Bridge at Niagara, breathing the spray of the unchanging Falls. He had seven days left.

They passed like a dream. He saw a great deal of the inner workings of the exec, more than before. He had privileges. He was up for membership in the club. Rosalie had proposed him. He talked with two Czechoslovakian ballet dancers in their persons, and a succession of heavily accented Russians and Poles and Japanese through the mouth of the beach boy who came to tend Rosalie's garden. He thought they liked him and was pleased that he penetrated where he had not been allowed before…until he realized that these freedoms were in themselves a threat. They allowed him this contact so that they could look him over. If they rejected him they would have to kill him, because he had seen too much. But by then a week had passed, and another day, and though he did not know it, he had only one day left. Rosalie did what she could to make the days of waiting easy for him.

"Embarrassing, isn't it? I went through it myself, love. Come have a drink."

205

"When will I know?" he demanded fretfully.

"Well." She hesitated. "I don't suppose there's any harm in telling you, love, under the circumstances—"

He knew what the circumstances were.

"I guess I can tell you. You need just over seven hundred votes to come in. You've got—" Her eyes glazed for a moment. She was looking through some clerk's eyes, somewhere on the island. "You've got about a hundred and fifty so far. Takes time, doesn't it? But it's worth it in the end."

"How many 'no' votes?"

"None," she said gently. "You'll never have but one, love, because that's all it takes."

He stared. The girl gook took up his hand and kissed it lightly. "One blackball's enough, yes, but never fear. Rosie's on your side."

RESTLESSLY Chandler stood up and made himself another drink. His head was beginning to buzz. They had been drinking on her sun terrace since early afternoon.

Rosalie came up beside him soothingly. "I know how you feel. Want me to tell you about when I went through it?"

"Sure," he said, stirring the ice around in the glass and drinking it down. He made another drink absently, hardly hearing what she said, although the sound of her voice was welcome.

"Oh, that lousy headdress! It weighed twenty pounds, and they put it on with hatpins." He caressed her absently. He had figured out that she was talking about the night New York was bombed. "I was in the middle of the big first-act curtain number when—" her face was strained, even after years, even now that she was herself one of the godlike ones—"when something took hold of me. I ran off the stage and right out through the front door. There was a cab waiting. As soon as I got in I was free, and the driver took off like a lunatic through the tunnel, out to Newark Airport. I tell you, I was scared! At the tollbooth I screamed but my—friend—let go of the driver for a minute, smashed a trailer-truck into a police car, and in the confusion we got away. He took me over again at the airport. I ran bare as a bird into a plane that was just ready to take off. The pilot was under control... We flew eleven hours, and I wore that damn feather headdress all the way."

She held out her glass for a refill. Chandler busied himself slicing a lime for her drink. Now she was talking about her friend. "I hadn't seen him in six years. I was just a kid, living in Islip. He was with a Russian trade commission next door, in an old mansion. Well, he was one of the ones, back in Russia, that came up with these." She touched her coronet. "So," she said brightly, "he put me up for membership and by and by they gave me one. You see? It's all very simple, except the waiting."

Chandler pulled her down on the couch beside him and made a toast. "Your friend."

"He's a nice guy," she said moodily, sipping her drink. "You know how careful I am about getting exercise and so on? It's partly because of him. You would have liked him, love, only—well, it turned out that he liked me well enough, but he began to like what he could get through the coronet a lot more. He got fat. A lot of them are awfully fat, love," she said seriously. "That's why they need people like me. And you. Replacements. Heart trouble, liver trouble, what can they expect when they lie in bed day in and day out, taking their lives through other people's bodies? I won't let myself go that way... It's a temptation. You know, almost every day I find some poor woman on a diet and spend a solid hour eating cream puffs and gravies. How they must hate me!"

She grinned, leaned back and kissed him.

Chandler put his arms around the girl and returned the kiss, hard. She did not draw away. She clung to him, and he could feel in the warmth of her body, the sound of her breath that she was responding. The drink made him reckless; the last two weeks made him doubtful; he was torn. He could tell that there was no resistance in her body, but the coronet made it in doubt; she could fling him away from her with one touch of the mind. Yet she didn't do it—

"*Vi myenya zvali?*" his own voice demanded, harsh and mocking.

THE GIRL tried to push him away. Her eyes were bright and huge, staring at him. "Andrei!"

"*Da, Andrei! Kok eto dosadno!*"

"Andrei, please. I know that you are—"

"Filthy!" screamed Chandler's voice. "How can you? I do not allow this carrion to touch you so—not vot is mine—I do not allow him to live!" And Chandler dropped her and leaped to his feet. He fought. He struggled; but only in his mind, and helplessly;

his body carried him out of the room, running and stumbling, out into the drive, into her waiting car and away.

He drove like a madman on roads he had never seen before. The car's gears bellowed pain at their abuse, the tires screamed.

Chandler, prisoned inside himself, recognized that touch. Koitska! He knew who Rosalie Pan's lover had been. If he had been in doubt his own voice, raucous and hysterical with rage, told him the truth. All that long drive it screamed threats and obscenities at him, in Russian and tortured English.

The car stopped in front of the TWA facility and, still prisoned, his body hurried in, bruising itself deliberately against every doorpost and stick of furniture. "I could have smashed you in the car!" his voice screamed hoarsely. "It is too merciful. I could have thrown you into the sea! It is not painful enough."

In the garage his body stopped and looked wildly around. "Knives, torches," his lips chanted. "Shall I gouge out eyes? Slit throat?"

A jar of battery acid stood on a shelf, *"Da, da!"* screamed Chandler, stumbling toward it. "One drink eh? And I von't even stay vith you to feel it, the pain—just a moment—then it eats the gut, the long slow dying…" And all the time the body that was Chandler's was clawing the cap off the jar, tilting it—

He dropped the jar, and leaped aside instinctively as it splintered at his feet.

He was free!

Before he could move he was seized again, stumbled, crashed into a well—

And was free again.

He stood waiting for a moment, unable to believe it; but he was still free. The alien invader did not seize his mind. There was no sound. No one moved. No gun fired at him, no danger threatened.

He *was* free; he took a step, turned, shook his head and proved it.

He was free and, in a moment, realized that he was in the building with the fat bloated body of the man who wanted to murder him, the body that in its own strength could scarcely stand erect.

It was suicide to attempt to harm an exec. He would certainly lose his life—except—that was gone already anyhow; he had lost it. He had nothing left to lose.

CHAPTER FOURTEEN

CHANDLER loped silently up the stairs to Koitska's suite.

Halfway up he tripped and sprawled, half stunning himself against the stair rail. It had not been his own clumsiness, he was sure. Koitska had caught at his mind again, but only feebly. Chandler did not wait. Whatever was interfering with Koitska's control, some distraction or malfunction of the coronet or whatever, Chandler could not bank on its lasting.

The door was locked.

He found a heavy mahogany chair, with a back of solid carved wood. He flung it onto his shoulders, grunting, and ran with it into the door, a bull driven frantic, lunging out of its querencia to batter the wall of the arena. The door splintered.

Chandler was gashed with long slivers of wood, but he was through the door.

Koitska lay sprawled along his couch, eyes staring.

Alive or dead? Chandler did not wait to find out but sprang at him hands outstreched. The staring eyes flickered; Chandler felt the pull at his mind. But Koitska's strength was almost gone. The eyes glazed, and Chandler was upon him. He ripped the coronet off and flung it aside, and the huge bulk of Koitska swung paralytically off the couch and fell to the floor.

The man was helpless. He lay breathing like a steam engine, one eye pressed shut against the leg of a coffee table, the other looking up at Chandler.

Chandler was panting almost as hard as the helpless mass at his feet. He was safe for a moment. At the most for a moment, for at any time one of the other execs might dart down out of the mind-world into the real, looking at the scene through Chandler's eyes and surely deducing what would be no more to his favor than the truth. He had to get away from there. If he seemed busy in another room perhaps they would go away again. Chandler turned his back on the paralyzed monster to flee. It would be even better to try to lose himself in Honolulu—if he could get that far—he did not in his own flesh know how to fly the helicopter that was parked in the yard or he would try to get farther still.

But as he turned he was caught.

CHANDLER turned to see Koitska lying there, and screamed.

His eyes were staring at Koitska. It was too late. He was possessed by someone, he did not know whom. Though it made little enough difference, he thought, watching his own hands reach out to touch the staring face.

His body straightened, his eyes looked around the room, he went to the desk. "Love," he cried to himself, "what's the matter with Koitska? Write, for God's sake!" And he took a pencil in his hand and was free.

He hesitated, then scribbled: *I don't know. I think he had a stroke. Who are you?*

The other mind slipped tentatively into his, scanning the paper. "Rosie, you idiot, who did you think?" he said furiously. "What have you done?"

Nothing, he began instinctively, then scratched the word out. Briskly and exactly he wrote: *He was going to kill me, but he had some kind of an attack. I took his coronet away. I was going to run.*

"Oh, you fool," he told himself shrilly a moment later. Chandler's body knelt beside the wheezing fat lump, taking its pulse. The faint, fitful throb meant nothing to Chandler; probably meant nothing to Rosie either, for his body stood up, hesitated, shook its head. "You've done it now," he sobbed, and was surprised to find he was weeping real tears. "Oh, love, why? I could have taken care of Koitska—somehow—No, maybe I couldn't," he said frantically, breaking down. "I don't know what to do. Do you have any ideas—outside of running?"

It took him several seconds to write the one word, but it was really all he could find to write. *No.*

His lips twisted as his eyes read the word. "Well," he said practically, "I guess that's the end, love. I mean, I give up."

He got up, turned around the room. "I don't know," he told himself worriedly. "There might be a chance—if we could hush this up. I'd better get a doctor. He'll have to use your body, so don't be surprised if there's someone and it isn't me. Maybe he can pull Andrei through. Maybe Andrei'll forgive you then— Or if he dies," Chandler's voice schemed as his eyes stared at the rasping motionless hulk, "we can say you broke down the door to *help* him. Only you'll have to put his coronet back on, so it won't look suspicious. Besides that will keep anyone from occupying him. Do that, love. Hurry." And he was free.

Gingerly Chandler crossed the floor.

He did not like to touch the dying animal that wheezed before him, liked even less to give it back the weapon that, if it had only a few moments of sentience again, it would use to kill him. But the girl was right. Without the helmet any wandering curi-himself. The helmet would shield him from—

Would shield anyone from—

Would shield Chandler himself from possession if he used it!

He did not hesitate. He slipped the helmet on his head, snapped the switch and in a moment stood free of his own body, in the gray, luminous limbo, looking down at the pallid traceries that lay beneath.

HE DID NOT hesitate then either. He did not pause to think or plan; it was as though he had planned every step, in long detail, over many years. Chandler for at least a few moments had the freedom to battle the execs on their own ground, the freedom that any mourning parent or husband in the outside world would know well how to use.

Chandler also knew. He was a weapon. He might die—but it was not a great thing to die, millions had done it for nothing under the rule of the execs, and he was privileged to be able to die trying to kill *them*.

He stepped callously around the hulk on the floor and found a door behind the couch, a door and a hall, and at the end of that hall a large room that had once perhaps been a message center. Now it held rack after rack of electronic gear. He recognized it without elation. It had had to be there.

It was the main transmitter for all the coronets of the exec.

He had only to pull one switch—that one there—and power would cease to flow. The coronets would be dead. The execs would be only humans. In five minutes he could destroy enough parts so that it would be at least a week's work to build it again, and in a week the slaves in Honolulu—somehow he could reach them, somehow he would tell them of their chance—could root out and destroy every exec on all the islands.

Of course, there was the standby transmitter he himself had helped to build.

He realized tardily that Koitska would have made some arrangement for starting that up by remote control.

He put down the tool-kit with which he had been advancing on the racks of transistors, and paused to think.

He was a fool, he saw after a moment. He could not destroy this installation—not yet—not until he had used it. He remembered to sit down so that his body would not crash to the floor, and then he sent himself out and up, to scan the nearby area.

There was no one there, nobody within a mile or more, except the feeble glimmer that was dying Koitska. He did not enter that body. He returned to his own long enough to barricade the door—it had a strong-looking lock, but he shouldered furniture against it too—and then he went up and out, grateful to Rosalie, who had taught him how to navigate in the curious world of the mind, flashing across water, under a mind-controlled plane, to the island of Hilo.

There *had* to be someone near the stand-by installation.

He searched; but there was no one. No one in the building. No one near the ruined field. No one in the village of the dead nearby. He was desperate; he became frantic; he was on the point of giving up, and then he found—someone? But it was a personality feebler than stricken Koitska's, a bare swamp-fire glow.

No matter. He entered it.

AT ONCE he screamed silently and left it again. He had never known such pain. A terrifying fire in the belly, a thunder past any migraine in the head, a thousand lesser aches and woes in every member. He could not imagine what person lived in such distress; but grimly he forced himself to enter again.

Moaning—it was astonishing how thick and animal-like the man's voice was—Chandler forced his borrowed body stumbling through the jungle. Time was growing very short. He drove it gasping at an awkward run across the airfield, dodged around one wrecked plane and blundered through the door. The pain was intolerable. He was hardly able to maintain control.

Chandler stretched out the borrowed hand to pick up a heavy wrench even while he thought. But the hand would not grasp. He brought it to the weak, watering eyes. The hand had no fingers. It ended in a ball of scar tissue. The left hand was nearly as misshapen.

Panicked, Chandler retreated from the body in a flash, back to his own; and then he began to think.

It was, it had to be, the creature he had seen in the village of the dead. A leper. One of the few who escaped from the colony at Molokai. Chandler drove himself back to that body and, though it could not work well, he could make it turn a frequency dial, using its clubbed hands like sticks. He could make it throw a switch. He then caused it to place the toothed edge of a rusting saw on the ground and strike at it with its throat in a sort of reverse guillotine. Chandler could not see that he had a choice; he dared not have that creature left where it might be seized the moment he quit its body. It was better dead.

After that it all became easy.

In his own body he destroyed the installation in Oahu. A few minutes at Koitska's work bench, and he had changed the frequency on his own coronet to transmit on the new band the leper's touch had given the Hilo equipment.

He worked rapidly and without errors, one ear cocked for the sound of someone coming to threaten what he was doing (the sound never came), impatient to get the job done.

He was very impatient, for when he was done he would be the only exec.

And the execs would be only slaves.

CHAPTER FIFTEEN

CHANDLER strolled out of the TWA building, very tired.

It was dawn. His job was done. He carried the coronet, the only working coronet in the world, in his hand. He had spent the night killing, killing, killing, and blood had washed away his passions; he was spent. He had killed every exec he could find, in widening circles from the building where his body lay. He had slit his dozen throats and fired bullets into his hundred hearts and hundred brains; he had entered bodies only long enough to feel for a coronet, and if it was there the body was doomed; and he stopped only when it occurred to him he wasn't even doing that much any more. He had probably killed some dozens of slaves, as well as all the execs in reach. And when he stopped the orgy of killing he had made one last search of the nearer portions of the island and found no one alive, and he had then realized that one of the closest execs had been Rosalie Pan.

He knew that in a while he would feel very badly for having killed that girl (which could she have been? The one with the shotgun in the mouth? The one whose intestines he had spilled with a silver letter opener in a whim of hara-kiri?), but just now he was too worn.

He was Chandler the giant killer, who had destroyed the creatures who had destroyed a world, but he was all tired out. He poked at the filigree of the coronet absently, as a man might caress the pretty rug, which once had been the skin of a tiger that almost killed him. It was all that was left of the exec power. Who held this single coronet still held the world.

Of course, said a sly and treasonable voice in a corner of his mind, the job was not really done.

Not quite. Not all.

The job would not be done until it was impossible for anyone to find enough of the installations to be able to reconstruct them.

And then, said the voice, while Chandler stared at the dawn, listening, what about the *good* things the exec had done? Would he not be foolish to throw away so casually this one, unique chance to right every imaginable wrong the world might do him?

Chandler went back into the building and brewed some strong black coffee. While it was bubbling on the stove he slipped the coronet back atop his head. Only for a while, he promised. A very little while. He pledged himself solemnly that it would be just long enough to clean up all loose ends—not a moment longer, he pledged. And knew that he was lying.

THE END